VALIANCE

VALIANCE

VANESSA CARAVEO

Published in Los Fresnos, TX, U.S.A.

ISBN: 978-1-7333798-2-3 (Paperback)

Library of Congress Control Number: 2019918820

This is a work of fiction. Names, characters, businesses, places, events, locales, and incidents are either the products of the author's imagination or used in a fictitious manner. Any resemblance to actual persons, living or dead, or actual events is purely coincidental.

Ordering Information:
For details, contact the publisher at the address below.

Vanessa Caraveo
P.O. Box 93
Los Fresnos, TX, 78566

Printed in the United States of America

First Edition

First Printing, 2019

This book is dedicated to my mother, Elena,
and to the memory of my grandfather, David,
whose loving spirit sustains me still.

I am eternally thankful to both of you for always encouraging
me to believe in myself and
my ability to achieve whatever I aspired.

With Love,
Vanessa

Success is not measured by what you accomplish, but by the opposition you have encountered, and the courage with which you have maintained the struggle against overwhelming odds.

— Orison Swett Marden

PROLOGUE

How did I get here? I wondered as I stood in the lineup, my hand against my heart as the national anthem was sung. My heart was beating fast against my palm—not from nervousness or fear but from anticipation. Soon it would start, and I would be in my element. Nothing other than the ball and winning would matter to me.

This all started fourteen years ago on a hot afternoon in which I got lost when I was just four years old. My sister, Margarita, was supposed to pick me up from preschool, but I figured she had forgotten about me, so I tried going home by myself. Instead, I ended up wandering to the park, where I saw my first-ever soccer game in real life.

Soccer is not just a game; someone on TV said. *It is a way of life; it has a way of connecting people.* Margarita laughed before changing the station, but I took those words I had read on TV to heart.

I was four years old when I saw my first friendly neighborhood soccer match between two teams in their late teens. The game was just starting when I got there. I stood behind the fence, watching from the beginning to the end; that was how fascinated I was. I remained standing for the second match, immersed in it. Although there were words and terms I could not yet understand because I didn't know them at such a young age, I read the words at the bottom of the TV screen thanks to the closed captioning system I would activate with the remote control. I always enjoyed reading what the sports commentators said about the game and seeing their reactions on their faces when a goal was scored.

Margarita found me still standing there in the evening, watching the third match. She had been crying because Mom had scolded her. Margarita hit me on the back of the head when she saw me.

"Never, ever do that again," she warned, squatting before me and gripping me by the shoulder.

I just nodded.

Mom had been crying as well, and she hugged me tightly before she started scolding me. I didn't mind the scolding; I was lost in my thoughts, replaying the game over and over in my head. The next day at recess, I kicked about an empty bottle of water, trying to replicate the feeling of wonder I had felt the previous day.

Some of the children had laughed at me, but I didn't mind in the slightest. It was just me and my imaginary ball, and the world only came back to me when I stopped playing.

I played with my pretend ball on my way home from school. Margarita walked by my side and scowled at me with annoyance. She poked at me several times, but I paid no attention to her. I figured her frustration with me had reached its limits because she suddenly kicked the ball viciously into the street, a car running over it almost instantly. I stood there in disbelief, looking at the flattened piece of rubber that had been my beloved ball and slowly came out of my haze.

I looked up at Margarita and saw something that resembled regret flash in her eyes, but she stuck her tongue out at me.

"Come on," she growled, seizing my hand. She dragged me home, but our parents were not there. Complacently, Margarita left me to play in the living room while she went to sleep.

I found another pretend ball, Dad's empty beer can. Margarita was supposed to be watching me, but I took advantage of the fact that she was sleeping. I slipped out of the house and kicked my makeshift ball around our back yard. I didn't stop there; I went out to the curb. Immersed in my contentment, I soon got lost, not realizing I had wandered far from home and made it to the park.

There was a group of kids playing this time around, and they saw me watching them and beckoned me over.

"Hey, wanna play with a real soccer ball?"

Margarita came to find me again. Although she was frantic and said harsh words, nothing she said could steal the joy from me.

Before my fifth birthday, Mom asked what I wanted as a gift. I told her I wanted a soccer ball of my own. She smiled and told me she would see what she could do; it was a promise that incensed Margarita.

"Why does Diego have to get everything?" she asked. Her birthday had been a few months ago, and our parents hadn't had the money to buy her the doll she wanted or even a birthday cake.

Mom was unable to say anything. When I went to sleep, I dreamed about the soccer ball I had asked for.

She kept her promise and bought me a soccer ball, and Dad played soccer with me for a while on my birthday. Mom later took me to the park to play with the other kids, and together, we broke in my new ball. Those hours were the happiest of my life; I had finally found something I enjoyed. I wasn't a freak as my classmates had labeled me. Later that day, I went to sleep with the ball, and to my travesty, I woke to find it deflated, a shiny pair of scissors protruding from it.

Mom punished Margarita for her devilish act. Though she vehemently denied doing it, we knew it had been her. The look in her eyes when I'd unwrapped the ball had been pure spite. Mom stopped giving her allowance to save up to buy me a new ball.

When I was eight, I tried out for the junior soccer team. Soccer had become my passion, and I thought if it were taken from me, I wouldn't survive without it. I tried out for the team, but I wasn't accepted. The coach had given me a lot of excuses, none of which made sense to me. Mom made tacos to cheer me up. Margarita sneered while singing me the words *"lero, lero, lero,"* from a childhood mocking song in Spanish. Mom told her to leave, but Margarita said one last thing before she merrily skipped away.

"You're going to give up just because they said no to you once?"

Her words stuck with me, and I tried again. My new soccer ball lasted until middle school, when Miguel, my younger brother, kicked it across the street into the yard of Mr. Blanchett, our mean neighbor, who promptly confiscated it. We didn't tell Mom about it; she would have our hides if she found out we had disturbed one of Mr. Blanchett's meditation sessions.

We pooled our allowance to buy a new one before she noticed its absence, praying that Mr. Blanchett wouldn't come to tell Mom about what we had done. We shouldn't have bothered; unbeknown to us, Mr. Blanchett suffered from social anxiety and had a tremendous fear of leaving his home. Miguel borrowed the ball so he could play with his friends in the park. Sometimes I played with him and his friends. They always argued about which team I should be on, and occasionally I was the referee, something I oddly enjoyed. Margarita would occasionally come to watch us play in the park, mocking us. Without a doubt, she was very good at that.

By then, I still hadn't been accepted onto my school's team, but it was not for lack of trying. They had nothing against the way I played, even telling me I was a fantastic soccer player. Even with my evident skill, they just couldn't let me on the team. It was hard not to be disheartened. Sometimes, the disillusionment snuck up on me, and whenever it did, I thought about Margarita's words. I wasn't going to give up just because they said no.

I was thirteen and a freshman when I knew all I wanted to do was play soccer professionally. I had skipped a grade level in elementary school since I was considered a gifted student, so I was younger than my classmates were. On career day in school, they would talk to us about what we could be when we grew up and how we could make it possible. Mom wanted me to be a doctor. Although I never contradicted her, what I wanted most in life was to play soccer like Lionel Messi. I wanted to be on a soccer field, surrounded by my teammates, dribbling before adoring crowds. While all the other kids chattered about what they wanted to be, I never brought up what my greatest aspiration was—maybe out of fear I would jinx it.

"You can be whatever you want to be, Diego," Mom said. "The sky is your only limit."

I took her words to heart.

"Give up, Diego," the coach told me at my fourth try out. He was exasperated with my being there. "You aren't going to make the team. Just take up poetry or pottery. Soccer isn't for

5

you."

No matter how discouraging the words were, I did not allow them to stop me.

I had just turned fourteen when I learned of Simon Ollert, a German soccer player. Like me, he was born deaf in both ears and used hearing aids. I had read an article about him in a sports magazine someone had left lying around, having picked it up to take my mind off the continual rejection. He had made his professional soccer debut on September 16, 2014, my thirteenth birthday. What I read about him energized me; someone like him playing soccer professionally gave me hope that I could achieve my goal. I couldn't give up now that I had found I wasn't alone in my struggles.

I wouldn't take no for an answer, and I persevered through college. Now here I was, before the adoring crowd and part of the team representing the United States in the FIFA U-20 World Cup, surrounded by my teammates. I had distinguished myself before them, and they welcomed me as one of theirs. I was ready to show the world what I was made of.

CHAPTER 1

I was born on September 16, 2001. Mom said I came into this world five days after the 9/11 terrorist attacks that had destroyed the World Trade Center. To this day, I often shudder at the thought of having come into the world at a time when the United States had recently been rocked by such a horrific event. When I became old enough to understand, Mom explained the catastrophic event to me with the aid of gestures. I could never forget the horrors on her face every time she recounted the heart-wrenching story of what had transpired. Every time Dad and his American friends met for a night out, there was always something that nudged them into talking about the tragedy.

Dad was quite friendly to those who weren't his family, and it didn't take him long to become endeared to the locals who found him amusing. They even insisted on learning whatever bits of Spanish he could teach them, and he was more than willing to share his roots with them. When they didn't come to the house, they'd go out to have a drink together. Dad never got drunk, though; a drink or two, and he was good.

Mom and Dad had immigrated to Sacramento two years before I was born. According to my older sister, Margarita, they used to live on a very rowdy street in Ixtepec, a small city in the state of Oaxaca in Mexico. I had often wondered if it faced a mountain or had a view of a hill as its translation from Nahuatl suggests. She was three by the time Mom and Dad moved to the United States, so I doubted she remembered anything about their old home.

Back to the day on which I was born. Mom told me I arrived four days earlier than expected. I was a large baby, so she had undergone a lot of pain, but she finally gave birth to me with a broad smile on her face. She named me Diego, after Juan Diego, the first Roman Catholic indigenous saint. It was quite ironic being named after a man who had Cuauthtlatoatzin, loosely translated as *The Talking Eagle,* as a birth name. She said I would never abandon her, just as James of Zebedee had always stayed true to Christ. I had never understood that part until today.

While everything was perfect after my birth, the sad news about my reality came three days later. I was born deaf and with an extremely rare congenital anomaly that impedes me from being able to produce sounds with my vocal cords. I would have to live the rest of my life dependent on hearing aids and sign language to be able to communicate. It isn't that bad now, actually. I've learned to live my life as a teenage boy reading people's lips more than relying on battery-powered electronic devices affixed to his ears.

For years, Mom didn't take the news well. She kept me close to her, paying rapid attention to what I wanted or needed. It's been years, but I can still remember her loud yelp when I tripped from a swing at the age of three and hurt my knee. Although I had hearing aids, she made sure I never walked alone or stepped close to the busy streets of Sacramento. I always felt safe with her at my side.

It wasn't all sunshine and rainbows in Sacramento for an undocumented family who had two young mouths to feed. Now that I am almost eighteen, I realize today that Mom had sacrificed a lot by keeping me close all the time. She worked the morning shift at a local supermarket in downtown Sacramento and then worked in the evenings at another supermarket on 30th Street. More often than not, her street smarts kept her safe. She couldn't afford to be found loitering in downtown Sacramento, especially in Granite Regional Park beyond work hours. The risk of being mugged or something worse happening was a constant reality because of the high crime levels in the neighborhood.

Mom would take me to work, keeping me in a small crib close to her. Her manager often snapped at her because she would frequently pause what she was doing to check up on me, and sometimes customers would get impatient and leave. By the time I was three and a half, she kept me at home with my younger brother, Miguel. Our sister Margarita would watch over us. Mom always hurried to get back home to prepare lunch and dinner and tuck us into bed.

The earliest memory I have of my sister was when she told me about our home in Mexico. Margarita loved telling us stories, and I managed to follow by paying attention to her lips as she spoke. Mom and Dad didn't have the money to renew the old hearing aids they had bought for me when I was a toddler, so sometimes it was difficult for them and Margarita to know whether my hearing aids were working or not. I was four then, and she had just celebrated her tenth birthday on July 27. We both sat in the middle of the room, facing each other and holding hands.

"Our old home was almost as small as this one," Margarita explained. "Mom didn't always work in a supermarket. She used to sell fruit juices and snacks."

I gestured to Margarita with signs I knew she could understand, eager to find out what kinds of juices and snacks Mom used to sell.

She bit her lips for a moment as she thought. "Aguas frescas, palomitas, and limonada."

I didn't know what any of those things were, but I nodded, gesturing, "Are those snacks tasty?"

"Yes, they are. Sometimes, late in the night, children would come to knock on our door to ask Mom if she could sell some to them."

"And would she?" I motioned with my hands.

"She didn't have a choice. They would keep knocking and knocking, disturbing Dad until she came to the door and sold them some."

"What about Dad? What did he do in Mexico?"

"Oh, I can't remember, but he would always come home stained with dirt."

I gleamed gleefully. "Maybe Dad was a mechanic!" I gestured, blinking in excitement.

"No… or maybe he was," Margarita responded skeptically. "I thought I was the one telling you how it was before we came to the United States? You weren't there!"

I placed my hand over my lips, suppressing an amused face. She snorted and tapped my head. "Oh, you—you…" she growled.

Sorry, I gestured with beady eyes.

Margarita was bossy; I had known that about her from a very young age, and I hardly argued with her about anything. I also knew she didn't like it when Mom placed too much attention on me, and perhaps that made her jealous, but now, I realize she really couldn't change anything about herself.

Another earlier memory of Margarita was when she cooked

pozole with Mom in the kitchen. They had spent a lot of time there, slicing and shredding chiles, garlic, oregano, and cumin, while Dad and I watched TV. Dad hardly ever said a word; he would sit down and quietly stare at everything happening around him. It was as if Mom was head of the family, while he quietly slipped in and out of the house as he wished. There were times when my hearing aids enabled me to faintly hear what was on the television and the sound of my parents, Margarita or Miguel.

As my hearing aids no longer functioned well, the sound they transmitted would continuously fade in and out. As a result, I had to read people's lips when they were speaking and rely on their facial expressions and gestures. In between reading their lips and deciphering what they were saying from what sounds did manage to get transmitted through the hearing aids, I could make sense of what people were saying or what they wanted me to do.

Whenever I tapped and gestured to Dad wanting to know who the people on the TV were, he would only shake his head and explain I would understand everything when I was older. When he simply glanced at me with an annoyed expression on his face, I would deduce that it must have been because I was asking too many questions. If I dared to persist, he would yell out, "¡Silencio!" and that would keep me quiet for the rest of the day. I had become so accustomed to reading his lips and body language that I could immediately decipher when he wanted me to be quiet. Dad could have quite a bad temper. When I was older, I would find out Mom and Dad had their fair share of problems.

I realized very early in life that Mom found it difficult to talk about how she had learned about my disability at birth. As a child, I never quite understood why she always changed the subject or left the room whenever I directed the conversation towards that particular topic. Even today, I still don't understand why she acts like some parents do when their young children catch them off guard with questions they're not yet prepared to answer.

I finally got her to talk about it on my fourth birthday. Margarita and I had been communicating about our former house in Mexico, and she had been regaling me with tales. Even at that young age, I was already quite aware she probably couldn't remember most of the events considering she was just three years old when our parents had left Mexico, but I still paid attention to her every word and movement.

Mom was quite the storyteller, which is from where Margarita had inherited her ability. It was one of those lucky days when my hearing aids worked, so I was incredibly happy.

"Tell us more about it, Mom," I motioned to her, and Margarita also lent her voice to my request.

Her smile told us she was enjoying the attention she was getting from us. Mom then adjusted her flared skirt as she sat on the couch next to me. She pulled me toward her and then patted my hair in the affectionate way I loved.

"It was a very rigorous journey," she said before sighing dramatically.

Margarita and I chuckled.

"And when we got here, everything was different than what we were expecting."

"What do you mean?" Margarita asked.

"I was stunned by how everything was so beautiful!"

I hadn't yet been to any other country then, but from the little I had seen of the uptown area of Sacramento, I was pretty sure the skyscrapers in the uptown areas topped the list of the most beautiful buildings in the world. We lived in a downtown ghetto, and I thought the buildings there, including ours, were extremely ugly compared to the ones I had seen in the nice neighborhoods and on television.

"This country is a lovely place to live, and even more so if you're wealthy," she continued. "We eventually moved into this house, and our family grew. Would you believe if I told you both that I never went to the hospital for scans or checkups until it was time for delivery?" she said in a conspiratorial tone.

I didn't exactly understand what a scan meant, but I could see from her reaction that Margarita knew exactly what Mom was talking about. Gasping, she asked Mom, "Why?"

"Are you kidding? Your dad and I were illegal immigrants, and we were petrified. We'd heard tales of how people had been deported after getting caught by the government. We didn't want that to happen to us, so our best bet was to stay at home and hope nothing went wrong."

Many years had passed since they had first arrived in the United States, and my young mind reasoned that my parents must both still be illegal since they always hid or seemed to get nervous whenever they saw a police officer or a police car.

"We had to take you to Valentino's family when I was close to giving birth to Dieguito," she said to Margarita.

Valentino was my uncle, who lived a few streets away from ours.

"By the time we finally headed to the hospital, I was in intense labor pain, and I prayed we'd get there before I gave birth in the car. As soon as we arrived, I was taken to the emergency room."

"But weren't you scared the government would discover you at the hospital?" Margarita asked.

Mom smiled. "We'd been informed by Karina that childbirth

was an emergency, so we didn't need any ID. Do you understand now?"

Margarita and I nodded, but most of what they said was too complicated for me to understand.

"There were no complications, so we were preparing to be released from the hospital on the third day," she sighed. "But just before being discharged, they were conducting more tests on the adorable, chubby little Diego. That's when things suddenly changed."

I tapped Mom in a frenzy, shock rippling through me. "You were caught by the government!" I signed, eager to know what had happened.

"No, silly," Margarita replied, turning to me. "If they had been arrested, we would be in Mexico by now and not in the United States."

I frowned while giving thought to what my sister had said. I finally shrugged. She must be right. After all, she was older and knew a lot more than I did.

"We weren't caught," Mom said, her eyes welling up. "We've never been caught. Little Diego failed the hearing screening test."

There was an uncomfortable silence as Margarita stole a glance at me.

"According to the specialist, he'd used special equipment to play sounds in Diego's ears, but he hadn't responded accordingly," she said with a faraway look on her face. "I was scared... really scared; the doctor must have sensed it. He said the test results didn't necessarily mean Diego was deaf. He explained they might mean nothing, but they could also mean a great deal."

It had felt surreal, sitting there, watching Mom speak, deciphering her every word in between reading her lips, observing her movements and gestures, and listening to what little sound I managed to hear with my hearing aids. Learning about how she had given birth to me and the tragic circumstances that had followed had me completely captivated. The fact Mom never wanted to speak about the topic made it even more special.

"The doctor told us to come back after three weeks for a retest. Your father had agreed to it initially. Alejandro was just as worried as I was... if not even more. However, as the days progressed, your dad began to talk about how we didn't really need to go for a retest, especially since the doctor had said it might be nothing."

Margarita shook her head in distaste.

"Can you imagine that?" Mom said vehemently. "I didn't agree with your dad, of course. I can only imagine what would have happened if I hadn't returned to the hospital. According to him, he had spoken to some coworkers, and they all warned us we faced getting caught if we went back to the hospital. That seemed quite logical because now that we had a regular appointment and weren't being admitted for an emergency, the hospital staff would surely ask us to show ID."

I stared at my sister, who listened with rapt attention and then turned around to listen to Mom continue telling us the rest of the story.

"I didn't listen to him; he tried to talk me into not going to the hospital for the retest, but I refused. My son's hearing was more important to me than living in the United States. If we got deported for seeking medical help, then I would have no regrets. I told him that straightforwardly. He stopped speaking to me for two days before the test, but I didn't care."

She smiled. "Of course, I had a plan, but I didn't inform Alejandro. He hadn't cooperated with me, so I didn't see the need to tell him about it. I rented a fake ID from a woman in the neighborhood, and I used it to identify myself when I got to the hospital. Of course, I knew what I was doing was extremely risky and possibly dangerous, but as a mother, I would do anything for my children," she stated, patting me on the head.

"I was apprehensive about using the fake ID, but luckily no one suspected anything. They did the retest, and it revealed Diego was deaf. It was the result I had been expecting, but I was still devastated... so much so, I couldn't even hear everything the doctor was telling me. He recommended the cochlear implant, but it was too expensive, and even if it had been affordable, I wouldn't have done it. I couldn't fathom the thought of a baby going through a three-hour surgery."

She spun toward me with a loving smile on her face. "Diego didn't grow up like every other child. He was different from other children, and with hard work, I adjusted to meet his needs. When he was still a baby, we would try things to see if he would react. I recall a time when Alejandro turned the volume of the stereo up to its loudest, and Diego didn't even flinch."

She exhaled softly, a tinge of pain in her eyes. "It was obvious he was unable to recognize sounds... that he couldn't even hear the sound of our voices. He never once reacted to any noise, no matter how loud it was. He never once turned his head when your Dad and I fought and argued. I would speak to him all day, but he never reacted or smiled. I came to realize that not only could he not hear when we spoke to him, but he couldn't speak either."

The sound from my hearing aids kept on fading out, so I had to read her lips.

"Diego never said 'papa' or 'mama' like other children do. He was totally different, and he had different needs. Raising Diego was a little more challenging. With you, all I had to worry about was if I was going to get enough sleep. With Diego, I had to be attentive to his every need and keep an eye on him every second."

I leaned against her, soothing myself with her warmth.

She turned toward me and smiled, her eyes reassuring. "Not that I'm complaining. I enjoyed every moment of raising you, Dieguito, and I still do. I'm eternally grateful I followed my instincts and ignored other people's advice. You were about a year old when we were finally able to get you your hearing aids, and it made a world of difference," she said. "Well... before they started malfunctioning," she shrugged.

I made a funny face, mainly to ease the tension. I knew how guilty Mom felt over my hearing aids malfunctioning, but I understood. Getting a hearing aid wasn't as cheap as getting a burger, and Mom and Dad didn't have the money to buy all the things we needed.

I glanced at Margarita. It was then I realized she was fast asleep, drooling all over herself. I shook my head. She was quite a sight when she slept.

"Margarita!" Mom called.

Margarita sat up immediately and glanced around in a dazed manner.

"Go to your room," Mom instructed her. With a sullen expression, Margarita marched off to our room.

Later that night, I lay awake on my bed, following the fascinating movements of a spider crawling on the wall above the dresser. My hearing aids had stopped working again, and my mind was clouded with thoughts.

I wondered if I was the reason Dad rarely participated in discussions in the house. His most active moments were those he spent in front of the TV. The rest of the time, when he was at home, he was usually asleep on the couch, drooling like Margarita.

Mom had admitted that my birth and the condition surrounding it had caused a strain on their relationship. While I was grateful to Mom for what she had done, I still felt a tiny bit of guilt. If only I had turned out like other kids, maybe Dad would stay at home more. Maybe he wouldn't look so sad and disgruntled all the time.

CHAPTER 2

I felt even guiltier when I finally got a new pair of hearing aids. Mom gave them to me just a few days before I was supposed to start kindergarten. It changed a lot of things. Not only did it improve my hearing, but it also made Dad even gruffer with me, and he kept to himself when he was at home.

I had a feeling the muffled arguments I heard in the days before I got my hearing aids was because Mom had spent a lot of money to buy me the new pair. When I asked Margarita, she simply shrugged in disinterest. She never seemed to care about what was going on at home. It made me wonder whether there was something wrong I knew nothing about.

Of course, Dad was not the only one who seemed upset by the new pair of hearing aids I had received. Margarita's eyes had widened in shock, envy, and bitterness. She refused to talk to me, even when I showed her the hearing aids and asked her what she thought of the green color.

The root of her waspishness was finally revealed when Mom called her to the kitchen to help prepare tamales for dinner. At first, she sat still and refused to respond even though I was able to hear Mom's call well enough, thanks to my hearing aids. I didn't call Margarita's attention to the fact Mom was asking her to go to the kitchen. Margarita had already snapped at me several times, and I didn't want her to do it again.

After calling her about five times, Mom finally came to the living room.

"You've been here all along, and you didn't respond to my call," Mom said, obviously annoyed.

Margarita shrugged. "I didn't hear you," she muttered under her breath.

I knew she was lying, but it was not my place to tell.

"Follow me to the kitchen now," Mom said. As she turned toward the kitchen, Margarita finally found her voice.

"Why can't Diego follow you to the kitchen?" she roared.

Mom turned around slowly, her eyes spitting fire. Mom was a loving person, but she was also the disciplinarian.

"What did you just say?"

Margarita lifted her head boldly and faced Mom. "You bought a pair of hearing aids for Diego, but you didn't buy me a new pair of shoes even though the ones I'm wearing to school are tight and uncomfortable."

I cringed, feeling sad and guilty. I felt guilty because Margarita hadn't gotten a new pair of shoes when she needed them while I had gotten the hearing aids. I felt tremendous sadness because I was pretty sure Margarita hated me now. I was also sure Mom was going to rain fire and brimstone on Margarita, so I couldn't help but pity her.

Margarita's boldness and outspokenness seemed to pay off because Mom turned back to the kitchen without saying a word. I glanced at Margarita, and she had a victorious smile on her face. I headed to the kitchen to help Mom, but she waved me back while angrily cutting the cabbage.

Margarita walked around the house with an extra spring in her step. She was so happy she even commented on my hearing aids.

"They look horrible... They're so ugly! Ugh!" She topped her comment off with a perfect demonstration of vomiting before walking away.

Of course, I didn't feel terrible. Actually, I did, but it was because of the guilt I felt, not because of Margarita's acerbic comments and scathing insults. I understood her pain. She had always been envious of the fact that I got most of the attention, but there was absolutely nothing I could do to make her feel better.

I soon forgot about Margarita's actions, and I thought Mom had forgotten about it too until it was time for dinner. Mom served the meal onto our separate plates, and I was already on my second spoonful when...

"Wait!" Mom said, smiling mischievously at Margarita before she could savor her first bite.

I munched on my food slowly, wondering what was going on.

"What are you trying to do?" Mom asked.

Margarita blinked, obviously confused. I was also confused. Why was Mom asking such an unnecessary question?

"Can't you answer me?" Mom asked, obviously enjoying herself.

"I'm about to eat," Margarita said. She still had the fork raised to her mouth, and from the way she blinked rapidly, I knew she wanted nothing more than to down the food.

"What food?" Mom asked.

Margarita frowned. "This food." She held on stubbornly to the fork.

"The food I prepared and cooked, you mean?" Mom emphasized.

"Yes." Margarita nodded. I already had an idea of where Mom was going with this.

"Good. I guess I need to remind you that this food is the same one you refused to help with," she said.

Margarita's eyes widened in both shock and disappointment. She carefully lowered the fork while looking at Mom.

"I'm sorry, Mom," Margarita said with shame in her voice.

Food was probably the thing Margarita loved most in the world. She could never skip a meal for anything—not even when she was sick.

"You're sorry?" Mom asked. "I really don't think you are. You used your power and refused to help in preparing the meal, and now I've decided to use my power." She paused and raised her glass of water to her mouth.

Mom took her time to drink the water and then sighed. Margarita was close to tears. She looked at me, urging me to plead with Mom, but I continued munching away at my food. I was glad she wasn't having a happy meal. Margarita had made jest of my hearing aids, so I reasoned her punishment was well deserved.

"You will not be having dinner tonight," Mom said.

I gasped, and Margarita groaned in despair.

"Cover up your food and leave the dining table. Or, you can decide to stay and watch us eat, if you prefer," Mom said.

Margarita opened her mouth to talk, but closed it again. She peered at me, and I turned away in guilt. She glanced in Dad's direction, but he was quiet as usual, downing his dinner and minding his business. Of course, Margarita knew better than to call his attention to what was going on.

"Please, I—"

"Leave!" Mom said sternly. Her expression had changed.

Margarita blinked rapidly, sniffed, then rose cautiously from her chair and slouched away to our room.

Once she left, I pleaded with Mom, who shook her head.

"She's not eating tonight," she answered.

That night, I was unable to sleep. I was not the only one. Margarita kept tossing and turning, and the sound of her growling stomach told me hunger was keeping her awake. When I couldn't take it any longer, I snuck into the kitchen after making sure Mom was fast asleep, grabbed a ration of leftovers and put them onto a plate, got water, and took it all to our room.

I plunked down beside her on the bed and switched on the light. She was pleasantly surprised and even smiled sweetly at me.

"Thank you, Diego," she said.

I smiled proudly and watched her down the food.

Of course, I knew Mom was going to see the food had been tampered with, but I was going to deny it. There wasn't much she could do to catch the culprit.

"I was actually waiting for you to fall asleep so I could sneak to the kitchen and eat," she said with her mouth full.

No wonder she'd been tossing and turning on her bed.

As I'd expected, Mom asked who had tampered with the food the next day, but none of us owned up to it. She had stared long and hard at Margarita, but to my relief, she didn't do anything.

***

Even though I was quite apprehensive about leaving the house, I was very excited about my first day of kindergarten. I was going to turn five in just a few weeks, and I had been counting the days and months for this day to arrive. Although I was not five yet, Mom had applied for special permission for me to start early. The school principal had told Mom that I couldn't begin attending school until I had my new pair of hearing aids, so my first day of school had been delayed. Now that I finally had my new pair of hearing aids, I was all set.

I waited outside the office while Mom and the principal had a long talk. I could almost guess what the subject of their conversation was; that I was a special-needs student... and all those other things adults talk about.

Of course, Mom wanted me to go to a regular school, and while Dad repeatedly said I would do better at a special-needs school for the deaf, Mom stuck to her decision.

"My son is not going to go to a special-needs school just because he has difficulty hearing. A lot of deaf students attend schools for the hearing, and they do just fine there," she said.

Margarita told me all of this after eavesdropping on them at my insistence. I had been conscious of the fact they were talking about me, but I wanted to find out what they were saying exactly. Once again, I was glad Mom had spoken up for me. The fact that I was deaf definitely didn't mean I couldn't attend a regular school like every other regular kid.

That was what I thought—until my very first day of kindergarten! I got cold feet the instant I stepped into the classroom. School had resumed a week ago, but I had not been able to start because I had to wait for my new hearing aids. Now that I had them, I could start. I hoped and prayed I would make lots of friends.

Starting late meant every other student in the class had gotten the time and opportunity to familiarize themselves with each other, so I was the odd one out.

The teacher introduced me to the class, and instead of saying hello, I simply waved at my classmates while smiling as broadly as I could. Mom had told me to smile while being introduced to my classroom.

I could hear a faint murmuring sound as my peers stared at me. Of course, I knew I was the cause, and that made me even more nervous.

I caught some of what was being said as I walked over to my seat.

"He's deaf!"

"He's the reason we have this new machine in class."

"They rearranged the classroom because of him."

Those were a few of the statements my hearing aids captured and that I managed to understand.

The classroom had been arranged in a U shape. At the center of the classroom was a radio-like machine that I would later find out was an FM listening system.

I hadn't once wondered how I would be able to learn effectively in a class filled with hearing students. I had just taken it for granted there would be an interpreter who would be using sign language. I couldn't possibly be the only deaf student in my classroom—that was what my young, innocent mind had thought.

While I had already mastered the art of reading lips, doing so with unfamiliar people felt uncomfortable, and the fact that everyone tended to talk more slowly around me complicated things. It made it almost impossible for me to catch on to whatever was being said.

When the teacher finally began to teach, she started to talk into a handheld microphone. It was an absolute miracle when I started to hear what was being said directly in my hearing aids. I was so surprised I could hear her voice well enough with them.

While the hearing aids helped a lot in hearing others speak, they had their downsides. Since hearing aids are manufactured to help the deaf pick up sound, it was quite tricky for me to hear in a room filled with a lot of people... especially hearing people.

The hearing aids could pick up any sound no matter how minute, and it made distinguishing a particular sound quite tricky. Having multiple people talking at the same time made it very hard to take note of all that was being said. It was even harder for me to concentrate on the words of one person since I kept getting distracted by what was being said by the other people. With no way to shut down or isolate other sounds, it was really challenging to concentrate on just one sound.

While the teacher spoke into the microphone of the FM listening system, the system transmitted the sound directly into my hearing aids. That way, it wasn't polluted by other irrelevant sounds. Because of this, the sound I could hear in my hearing aids was crisp and clear, and I could actually understand what the teacher was saying. I was free from background noise, and that was a massive relief to me, as most of my classmates were always making mean remarks.

I was so fascinated and excited by the system, I told Margarita it would be nice if we got one too.

She laughed at me, and then said, "Now you really want us to starve just so you can get a fancy new listening device. Have you forgotten what happened when you got your hearing aids?"

Of course, I hadn't forgotten—she'd been denied a new pair of shoes and had almost gone dinnerless when she tried to protest. That threat stopped me in my tracks, and I never asked Mom to get the FM listening device. It was when I was older I realized just how stupid it would have been for us to get one of our own; not everyone could be with it at all times, and unless everyone had their own personal system—which was impossible since it was expensive—it was practically useless and ineffective.

While the FM listening device made hearing in class much easier for me, I still had other challenges and hindrances. The classroom was set up in a U shape, and I was placed at one of the extremes. Because my seat faced the window directly, and the teacher often had her back turned to it, the sun's rays would prevent me from being able to read her lips. Since I was still heavily reliant on the ability to read lips even with the FM listening system, I couldn't see the teacher's face and mouth clearly enough to read her lips. This made me have to rely heavily on what I heard from my hearing aid, which amplified a lot of sound from the classroom.

Learning would have been bearable and considerably easy if it weren't for another factor that limited my hearing. My seat was placed very close to the air conditioning unit, and it made sounds that were often picked up by my hearing aid. The fact that my hearing aids further amplified the sound of the air conditioning unit made the classroom almost unbearable for me.

Most days, I went home with a headache from the sound of the AC, and it could be quite frustrating.

"It must be the stress of starting at a new school," Mom told me when I got home with an unbearable headache for the fourth time in a week.

I didn't report what was happening to anyone at school. As the only deaf student in a class of hearing children, I was already feeling guilty about the several changes already made to the classroom to accommodate my needs. It was even harder since most of my classmates didn't like me. They had to deal with a lot of changes because of me, and they always reminded me about it.

I attended school daily even though I dreaded it because of the headaches and the fact that I couldn't read my teacher's lips.

Every school day ended with me learning very little, and I usually came home feeling sick from the air conditioning unit in the classroom.

Mom realized just how little I was learning when I took my first report card home. I had scored far below average in most of my subjects. She panicked. That night, Mom and Dad argued again in their bedroom, and Margarita told me that Dad wanted me taken to a special-needs school for deaf children. Mom had stood her ground as usual, and it had turned into a full-blown argument. I lay awake for several hours after midnight, unable to sleep. I hated it when they fought because of me.

Mom followed me to school the next day and spent what seemed like an eternity in the principal's office before emerging with puffy eyes. Like all children, it always upset me to see my mom cry. I felt awful, and my headache had worsened.

We were having dinner when Mom broached the topic, which was unusual because Mom and Dad never talked about things like that in our presence.

"Diego might have to go to a special-needs school for deaf children," Mom said.

Dad shrugged. "I guess I was right all along." There was a hint of a smile on his cheeks.

"My son won't be going to a special-needs school," Mom said vehemently.

Dad knew better than to reply.

"His grades are abysmal, and the school is suggesting we transfer him to a special-needs school to see if he does better," she said.

My heart pounded heavily in my chest. I might not have been really fond of my school, but I certainly didn't want to attend a special-needs school.

"I managed to negotiate with the principal to give him the chance of finishing the semester so we can see if there will be an improvement in his performance. He promised to let him stay permanently if his scores get better," she said, stabbing the food in her plate with her fork as she spoke.

"Can you imagine that? Diego isn't the worst-performing student in his class, but the principal mainly wants to have him removed because he has special needs."

Her voice had risen a notch. "Why doesn't he tell the hearing students who performed poorer than Diego to withdraw and go to another school? Why must it be my Diego?"

No one gave her a response.

She turned her attention to me. "Diego, you must make me proud by the end of the semester. I know there is discrimination against you by your teacher and the school principal, but you need to prove them wrong."

I shifted uncomfortably in my seat. There was undeniably discrimination against me in school, but it was not from my teacher or the principal like Mom believed. It was from my fellow classmates. I wanted to tell her, but I didn't.

"If you can show that your performance is better by the end of the semester, then you won't have to go to a special-needs school," she told me.

I nodded, then bit my lip before finally pointing out what I had been keeping in.

"Maybe if my teacher wasn't standing with her back to the window and if I didn't have to sit beside the air conditioner," I informed her, gesturing.

She dropped her fork with a clang. Her face was strained. "What?"

"I can't read the teacher's lips when she speaks with her back turned to the window, and the sound from the air conditioner often gets picked up by my hearing aids, causing me to have really bad headaches," I explained.

She smiled, ruffled my hair, and said, "I think I have to pay the school principal another visit tomorrow."

Like she had said, she paid another visit to my school the next day. The teacher was summoned to the principal's office, and another teacher continued to teach us until she returned.

Once my teacher returned to the classroom, after spending what seemed like ages in the principal's office, she changed my seat, and when she eventually taught us later in the day, she had her back to the board instead of the window.

My scores finally picked up, and at the end of the semester, I was one of the three students with the best grades. Mom beamed with pride and hugged me affectionately.

I would continue to excel in my studies throughout elementary school and middle school, graduating with honors as the top student of my class. Mom even baked me a cake and bought me a pair of Nike cleats when I skipped third grade, but they didn't survive more than a week. Margarita was so upset over the attention I had gotten that she poured bleach all over them when she was doing her laundry chore, having claimed she had mistaken it for stain remover and color booster. Mom was so angry with her that she grounded her, and she wasn't allowed to watch TV for a month. Although I never really made any friends as I had wished, I had a few acquaintances with whom I played ball during recess and lunch hour. I couldn't wait to begin high school so I could join the high school soccer team. A whole new chapter of my life was about to begin.

CHAPTER 3

I blinked rapidly.

"Do you want to kiss me?" she glared. She had an amused expression on her face, and while I wasn't exactly sure whether she was joking or not, I was quite taken aback. I wasn't attracted to her in any way, and I definitely didn't have any intention of kissing her.

I immediately shook my head.

"Then why are you staring at my lips?" she asked.

It was then I realized what was going on. She was a new student, so I understood why she was misconstruing my intentions. I smiled at her in apology, but she frowned back at me, her eyes glaring.

"Don't you know he's a dumb dude?" said my least favorite classmate, Sebastian, before the rest of his cronies started roaring with laughter.

"He looks it too," the new girl chipped in.

"Let's get out of here," Fernando said, pulling me away from the classroom.

Fernando was my best friend. Unlike Miguel and I, who were born in the United States, Fernando had immigrated to the States with his parents. In simpler terms, he was in constant fear that he and his family would be discovered and deported back to

Mexico, just like my parents and sister. Making friends wasn't a walk in the park for him either. Supposedly, his American friends often picked on him, threatening they would report him to the authorities to get him deported. Often, he cowered in fright at the sight of cops. He was, in many respects, the only friend that I could rely on: he had my back at all times, even when I couldn't respond to defend him.

I followed him immediately.

"I can't wait to punch that Sebastian dude in the face!" Fernando seethed as soon as we got out of the classroom. He was livid, and I wished I could do or say something to help him, but I couldn't.

I placed my hand on his shoulder to comfort him. While Sebastian was a big bully, I always tried very hard not to cross paths with him. Even though bullying was forbidden, it still occurred anyways. Sometimes it happened right under the nose of the teachers, but they would just turn blind eyes.

"And that girl, who does she think she is?" Fernando demanded.

"Let it go," I implored him, signing.

He shrugged. "I'm going to get back at him one of these days," Fernando said, curling his hand into a fist.

I was tempted to laugh. Fernando was quite small, and this made him a target for bullies like Sebastian and his crew. While I had a much bulkier frame, I was a target for Sebastian and his friends because I was deaf and one of the top three in my class.

"Let's go to the soccer field," Fernando announced.

I loved soccer. It was one of the few things that made me happy.

"What joy do you boys ever get from running after a ball on a field?" Margarita often asked. "It's completely pointless. You guys would be better off doing something more productive."

I would just chuckle and leave my little brother Miguel to respond.

"We also have female soccer players," Miguel would reply. Sometimes, he would ask her what joy she got from painting her face with makeup.

Back to the present. Fernando and I rushed to the soccer field, momentarily forgetting about our oppressor, Sebastian.

We finally left the soccer field twenty minutes later. We were just on our way back to the classroom when we saw a small crowd in the hallway, blocking our way.

"What's going on here?" Fernando demanded.

I moved closer to the crowd and tapped the nearest person. The next thing that happened was so fast, I could have sworn it was all in my imagination if my cheek wasn't hurting so badly. I had received a slap to the face.

"Why would you touch me?" she screamed. "Are you trying to grope me? Is that it?" She advanced menacingly toward me as I stepped back to avoid her.

We were beginning to attract a lot of attention. I wished I hadn't tapped her at all. In fact, if I had known she was the same girl who had asked if I'd wanted to kiss her a few hours ago, I would have steered clear.

"Are you out of your mind?" Fernando came to my rescue, stepping right in front of me.

His attempt at acting like a bodyguard failed woefully.

"And what are you going to do about it?" the girl asked, now standing right in front of Fernando and looking down at him, much taller than he was.

There were sniggers and laughter from the other students in the hallway. It was getting pretty embarrassing, and Fernando, being the stubborn dude he was, did not back down.

In my sixteen years of existence as a deaf boy, I've had my gestures and actions misconstrued, but never had I been physically assaulted because of them—until today.

I tapped Fernando and motioned at him for us to leave.

"No, I'm not leaving, man. She's just a stupid girl who prefers getting in people's faces instead of vocalizing her anger."

"You're the stupid one," the girl replied with equal heat.

I tapped Fernando again, but he shrugged my hand away.

"Say that again, and I'm going to—"

"What are you going to do?" a familiar voice said from the crowd. I stood defensively when Sebastian came out with his other bully friends. Fernando swallowed nervously.

"Whimper in the locker room while I push you around?" he asked, raising his brow. His friends guffawed.

The girl smirked as she looked down at Fernando. He tried to lurch forward, but I held him tightly.

"Let's leave," I admonished him, signing.

"That's right!" Sebastian said. "Obey your deaf and dumb friend. Get out of here!"

The smirk wiped off the girl's face as her eyes traveled to my hearing aid, and her expression softened. We locked eyes for a short moment before I averted mine. I gripped Fernando's hand and was pulling him away when...

"What's going on here?" the principal asked, looking sternly at every one of us.

"She slapped—"

I don't know what prompted me to do it, but I clasped my palm tightly over his mouth. Those who were there, including the new girl and Sebastian, glanced at us. Fernando tried to speak up, but I pressed my palm against his mouth even more firmly.

When no one replied, the principal ordered everyone to leave since it was well past time for us to be in class.

Fernando was in a horrible mood by the time we got back to the classroom. He kicked his chair, then turned to me.

"Why didn't you allow me to tell the principal what that girl did?" he asked.

"It's not worth it," I gestured. At that moment, she walked past me and gave me a strange look that was neither friendly nor hostile; it was a calculating one.

Fernando glared at her, and he quickly averted her stare. She walked over to where Sebastian and his friends were sitting. They all began to laugh.

"*¡Idiotas!*" Fernando seethed.

"Hello," a soft, familiar feminine voice introduced herself as we headed home.

Fernando and I turned around to see who it was.

"What do you want?" Fernando asked, glaring at the girl.

The girl who had slapped me three days ago was standing right behind us with a smile that could have been construed as a kind one, providing I hadn't already been at the receiving end of her anger.

"Hi!" she said, smiling cheerily.

"Let's go. She obviously doesn't know what she wants," Fernando said, pulling me with him as we turned away.

"Wait!" she insisted.

I stopped walking, but Fernando didn't.

"Come on!" he said when he looked back.

"Let's hear what she has to say," I motioned, replying to him.

He gave the girl a scathing look, then walked back toward us. "What do you want?" he demanded again.

She shifted uncomfortably and bit at her lower lip. Even though her body language indicated she was uncomfortable standing there, I didn't pity her in any way.

She stretched her hands toward me. "I'm Seema!"

She looked beautiful with her feminine features and long, black hair. I could barely conceal the fact that I found her attractive. Seema was Indian; she had a smile that could melt a stony heart.

She smiled broadly, gazing at me. Her hands were still stretched toward me, dangling in midair. I took a glance at them, then back at her face. I then shook my head.

Her face fell in disappointment. If she thought she could say hi to me and I would forget all that she had done, then she was a big joke.

Her hands plodded against her side.

Fernando cackled. "Yeah! That's right!"

She shifted uncomfortably again. "Can you help me ask whether he's mad at me?" she asked, turning to Fernando.

He gave her a scathing look. "You can ask him yourself, and yeah, he really is mad at you."

She looked at me and then averted her gaze almost immediately.

"I'm sorry for slapping you. It was a terrible thing for me to do," she said quietly.

I communicated with Fernando using sign language to ask him to convey my apologies to her.

He turned to her with a straight face and apologized on my behalf.

She glanced at me quizzically, then back at Fernando. "I had no idea he was de—I mean, that he has hearing problems and is unable to speak. I—"

"You can say it," Fernando snapped. "He's deaf."

She blinked rapidly, flustered. "I had no idea he's deaf. I was only trying to defend myself."

"Defend yourself from what?" Fernando said. He could have taken the words right out of my mouth.

"Well, I thought he was groping me... I—"

"No way!" Fernando retorted, looking at her with something close to disgust. "Why would you even think that?"

Frantically, I communicated my fears to Fernando.

"He wanted to know why there were so many people in the hallway," Fernando said.

She tilted her head. "Then why was he staring at my lips earlier? I guess I reacted a little too harshly, but he was acting weird and creepy. Staring at my lips and creeping up on me from behind."

Fernando once again spoke on my behalf. "He's deaf. Even though he's using hearing aids, he still needs to read people's lips to be able to decipher what's being said. That's why he was staring at your lips," Fernando informed her.

"Ohhh! I'm really sorry," she said to me. "I just thought you were like the other guys, the ones at the group homes who would always sneak up on me and try to grope me while..." her words trailed off as she gasped and clasped a hand over her mouth.

"I'm sorry. I shouldn't have said that. I should leave now. I will see you guys tomorrow."

With that, she hurried off without so much as a backward glance.

Fernando and I exchanged looks, and he shook his head. "That girl is a nutcase if you ask me."

I disagreed. "I don't think so," I gestured to him. "She must have gone through a lot to have been that defensive."

Fernando scoffed. "Nothing's wrong with her. She's just a violent and bitter person."

"You heard what she said about some guys at group homes groping her, right?" I tried to reason with him.

He shrugged. "Maybe you're right."

If there was one thing I loved about Fernando aside from his loyalty, it was his open-mindedness. We became friends in our freshman year, at first communicating with each other through notes. I was so happy to finally have a friend, the first thing I did was tell Mom and Margarita as soon as I got home.

"Invite him over," Mom had said, even more ecstatic than I was.

"You can't hurry friendship, Mom," Margarita said.

A few months after we became friends, Fernando had given me the most fabulous surprise on my birthday. He had wished me a happy birthday in sign language.

I was elated and felt beyond grateful. I knew the effort learning sign language required, and to communicate with me effectively, Fernando had gone out of his way to take ASL classes. No one, aside from Mom, Miguel, and Margarita, had ever taken that extra step to communicate with me better. Fernando and I had been communicating using sign language ever since.

When I got home a few minutes later, I was greeted with loud shouts coming from our house. I hurried inside to find Margarita in the middle of the living room, puffing a joint. Mom stood a few feet away from her, screaming at the top of her lungs.

"SO YOU'RE NOT GOING TO PUT THAT JOINT OUT, IS THAT SO, MARGARITA?" she screamed.

"Stop screaming at me," Margarita said calmly as she puffed on it again.

"GET OUT OF MY HOUSE!" Mom shrieked.

Margarita laughed hysterically. "This is Dad's house, not yours," she retorted.

Mom grabbed a glass cup and threw it at her. Margarita swerved at the last minute, and it hit the wall, shattering into countless pieces.

"Margarita, come with me," I signed to her, pulling her outside after me. She didn't even bother resisting me.

"I hope you weren't hurt?"

She shook her head. "Who does she think she is, telling me to leave the house when she doesn't even own it."

"There are shards of glass on your top," I said to her.

She peered down at her top, looking for the nonexistent shards of glass.

"I'm just kidding," I said to her.

She smiled, which is what I'd been aiming for.

"Let's take a walk."

She nodded.

With my schoolbag still on my back, Margarita and I walked down the street where we'd grown up. I took my time to look at the other houses, and they were definitely not any better than ours was. They were all whitewashed by the rain.

"When did you get back?" I signed to her in an attempt to put what I had just witnessed behind us.

"Just this afternoon," she replied.

I looked over at Margarita and almost shook my head in sympathy. She was a shadow of herself. She wore a black top that hung loosely on her frame, and her jeans were barely held up by a belt that was now too large for her.

Since Margarita had moved out of the house to go live with her boyfriend, Mike, a few months earlier, she had lost a lot of weight. She looked thin—too thin. I was very worried about her.

"Are you okay, Margarita?" I gestured, demanding an honest response from her.

She nodded and puffed again. "I'm fine."

There was an uncomfortable moment of silence between us. I didn't believe her.

"You don't believe me, do you?" she eventually asked, breaking the silence.

I shook my head. I didn't.

"I'm fine... actually, I'm not," she giggled.

"What's wrong?" I demanded.

"Mike and I aren't on good terms right now. So, I came here in the meanwhile, wondering if he'll call me back."

"How about work?"

The last time we'd texted each other, she informed me she had gotten a job as a hostess at a restaurant.

"Mike said the pay was too small for the stress, so I quit after the manager refused to give me a raise."

Margarita may have been older than me by a little more than five years, but she definitely was not as smart as she often claimed to be.

She had left home for college three years ago. A year ago, she came home to tell us that she was dropping out, to Mom's utter dismay. Even Dad, who never seemed to have anything to say, was scandalized by the news and blurted out angrily.

Margarita, on the other hand, was set in her ways, and wouldn't change her mind for anyone... not even Mom and Dad. Goodness knows they tried to do everything to help her. We had all tried to help her, but she was as stubborn as a rock.

"College is just an institution and it's definitely not for someone like me. I just never seem to understand anything. All I ever do is attend classes and study eight hours a day for courses I've have absolutely no interest in. Even Mike said it's just a rat race," she had told me.

I believed she was making yet another wrong decision, and I didn't hesitate to let her know what I thought. This was the first time we had seen her since she had moved out, and she seemed to be spiraling down into a train wreck. I was very worried about her and hoped we could do something to help her see the light. If only she could see how much we loved her and only wanted the best for her.

Dinner was tense. Mom kept shooting dark looks at Margarita as we tried to eat our *arroz con pollo*. Margarita was sharing stories of her adventures while Dad, Miguel, and I ate silently, wanting nothing more than to escape the dinner table.

Mom was in a strange mood that evening. Her mouth dripped cruel, barbed words poised to wound. Margarita's foray into the world beyond our little house in downtown Sacramento seemed to have helped her develop a thick skin. Those words bounced off her like tennis balls lobbing against a concrete wall. It didn't stop Mom from trying, though. Her eyes had an odd glitter in them that told she wasn't stopping anytime soon. She would wear her dark mood like a shroud for the rest of Margarita's stay.

"How's school, Diego? Is everything okay there?" Margarita asked me, a small smile playing on her lips.

"Fine," I gestured, accompanied with a shrug, hoping it would end there, but it didn't. Mom clung to Margarita's every word as though they were a cue to continue with her attack.

"Diego is an honor roll student," she bit out. "One of the top three students in his class. He will soon go to a good university, graduate, and get an excellent job. Unlike you!" she hissed.

I felt uncomfortable and wished I could have magically whisked myself out from there or by some act of divine intervention. There was nothing Margarita hated more than being compared to me, her younger brother, who had disabilities, and who was excelling at everything she'd failed. I placed my fork down and tried to chew the food in my mouth as I waited for the storm, but it was like chewing rubber. With a great force of will, I swallowed it. At the other end of the table, sitting directly across from Mom, Dad looked up from his plate. Our eyes met and locked for a moment before he looked away.

Margarita laughed, emitting a harsh, bitter sound.

"Dieguito, the wonder boy!" she said, a sneer of mockery in her voice. "Isn't it because you put so much pressure on him, eh, Mama? You focus solely on him and forget about me, Papa, and Miguel."

Mom flinched as though Margarita had slapped her across the face. The heat of her anger bled from her eyes. "That's not true, Margarita."

"Deny it all you want, Mama. It doesn't change the fact that Diego will soon be done with high school and go to college, but I won't be surprised if he gives up halfway through like I did when he's away from your incessant nagging."

I would have given anything in the world for Margarita to take that back so I wouldn't have to see the pale, stricken look on Mom's face. Her mouth opened and closed several times, but she had no retort. She slumped in her chair, gazing at Margarita as though she had never seen her before.

Margarita had a small smile of triumph on her face as she excused herself. Without looking back, she skipped outside. The slam of the door jolted us from the stupor we were in. Dad cleared his throat before also excusing himself.

Miguel was still gaping at Mom in befuddlement as to why she hadn't verbally ripped Margarita to pieces when she dared talk back to her. I tapped his forearm to get his attention, telling him to leave.

He went eagerly, carrying his half-full plate with him to the room. I waited until I saw the bedroom door close before I turned back to Mom. I rapped the table with my knuckles to get her attention, but she paid me no mind.

Pushing my chair back, I went around the table to sit where Miguel had just vacated. Her expression of deep pain made my heart clench.

"Diego, my Diego," she rasped, her eyes welling up with tears.

I leaned against her, resting my head on her forearm before she shifted and encircled me with her arm, bringing me closer. I told her not to let Margarita get to her, that they should both find a way to put the past behind them. Margarita's accusation had hurt her so much, I had to comfort her with my touch.

Mom cried, her tears falling into my hair. I hugged her tighter, wishing I could say soothing words to make her feel better. After a few minutes, Mom regained her composure and asked me to clear the dinner table. She was deep in thought as we washed and wiped side by side. She was still distraught when she kissed me goodnight. I went back to the room I shared with Miguel and found he was already asleep.

I lay on the bed, waiting for Margarita to come in so I could talk to her about Mom. There was an urgency in me to speak with her. Maybe I could get both of them to get along peacefully. Margarita didn't come back that night. I dozed off on the couch, my mind shifting from one thought to another. As I slowly drifted into sleep, Seema's smile was the last image on my mind.

CHAPTER 4

"Aren't you trying out for the soccer team anymore?" Fernando asked, fiddling with his Rubik's cube. He did that every time he was nervous or anxious, and this morning, he had enough reason to be both.

Usually, our walk to school every morning was pleasantly uneventful, and we would spend the fifteen minutes chatting. Fernando would come to my house, kicking the ball against the picket fence until I went out. He would say good morning to Mom, who sometimes stood behind me. From there, we would walk to Cutler High.

This morning started the same way. Fernando was telling me about a new video game his dad bought him when we spotted a patrol car with a hard-faced cop leaning against the fender, and the words shriveled and died on his lips. He immediately hunched his shoulders, trying to make himself appear smaller and less threatening. With his small and thin frame, glasses, and bowl haircut, he looked as non-threatening as they came.

Maybe it was the shifty, I-need-to-hide look on Fernando's face that made him suspicious of us. He whistled and motioned with his hand for us to come closer. We went to him with extreme reluctance and nervousness, Fernando even more so, as he kept trying to hide behind me. I wasn't as scared of cops as Fernando was, but I'd had my fair share of encounters.

"On your way to school?" the cop asked. His eyes were bottle green and just as expressionless.

I nodded, wondering what he wanted from us. He didn't look particularly threatening, but he didn't look friendly, either.

"Do you know Raquel?" he asked.

I shook my head, and he nodded as if that had explained something to him, and then he caught sight of Fernando sheepishly standing behind me, looking like a frightened mouse.

"What's the matter with him?" he asked with a puzzled frown.

"We have a calculus test this morning," I lied. The cop directed a frown to my signaling fingers. He then glanced up at my face, his eyes darting to my ears for the hearing aid that would convince him of my disability. He shifted uncomfortably before saying, "Stay in school, kids."

We reached the next block, long gone from the cop's sight, yet Fernando was still anxious. I was glad he was talking. Sensing he needed a distraction from his nerves, I started signing.

"I'll try again today. I have a plan to convince Coach Miller to let me on the team," I signed, confident my plan would work.

I had been trying to get onto a soccer team since I was eight and in elementary school. Fernando and I met in our freshman year and bonded over our brimming love for soccer and the sting of rejection we often encountered. The coach rejected Fernando because of his small frame, while the coach rejected me because he thought I would be a hindrance on the field instead of an advantage, never mind the fact that I scored all the shots. He told me some things about teamwork and communication that didn't get anywhere with me. I was angry and depressed as I slunk back to the bleachers to watch the rest of the tryouts, nursing my bitterness.

It was in times like that when I resented my abnormality as I saw it in the dark haze of my anger. I disliked how everyone treated me differently because I was both deaf and with the inability to use my vocal cords to communicate. It was harder to succeed at anything because I had to prove I was up to the task, and because no one gave me the chance to prove I could. I never shared these thoughts with anyone; Mom would scold me severely if she got the hint that my thoughts went down a dark tunnel.

I was deeply entranced in my whirlwind of negative thoughts when Fernando came to sit beside me on the bleachers, muttering about the coach. I turned to look at him, his face set in a sulky scowl as he swung his legs back and forth. I guessed I'd been staring hard enough for him to notice someone was watching him. He suddenly turned to face me, and I jumped, startled by the intensity of his gaze. He had been one of the few that hadn't been freaked out by my staring at his lips. He understood the situation almost immediately and grinned at me.

"Fernando, Fernando Cortez," he introduced himself, holding his hand out to me.

I mouthed my name to him, taking care to make it slow, and shook his hand.

It took several tries before he finally guessed my name. From there, he began to talk. Fernando could be quite talkative when he had the audience, and I was fascinated by the way he endlessly yammered. We walked each other home after school that day, and I discovered we lived on the same street; his house was at the end of the cul-de-sac. I had been beyond excited about having found a friend who didn't seem to mind the fact I was deaf and unable to speak. I was also nervous that things could be different tomorrow, that I would be friendless once again. Now that

I had found Fernando, going back to being a loner wasn't an option; the thought of losing him anguished me. Later in the evening, after having told Mom about my newfound friend, I brought up the painful subject of the tryouts and how the coach had denied me a place on the team.

Mom had smiled patiently, ruffling my hair, and told me no matter the opposition, I should always strive for my dream, and I did—no matter how many times the coach said no. After so many years, I was beginning to see cracks in his otherwise cold demeanor. I knew that with the proper plan, I could manage to convince him.

Soccer was my passion. Mom, Margarita, and Miguel thought it was a hobby. No one knew how deeply passionate I was about the game except for Fernando. It wasn't just a game to me; it was a way of life. I knew hard work, persistence, and determination on the field would ultimately pay off. I wanted to play in front of an adoring crowd chanting my name in a pulsing rhythm. I played with Fernando in his yard and on the field during lunch at school, but it wasn't enough for me. To me, it was the ultimate way of proving to myself that no obstacle, no disability, could prevent me from making my dreams come true. I'd had my eyes set on making the school's soccer team for a long while now. I wanted to be like Simon Ollert, the German soccer player. He was deaf, and he did not allow his disability to impede him from pursuing his greatest dream.

Once, Mom had taken me to a seminar for people with disabilities or challenges, as I preferred to call them. One of the speakers was a deaf criminal lawyer who was quite well known. She told us to turn our so-called difficulties into weapons. We should work hard to achieve our dreams not only because of our challenges but also in spite of them. Those words had stuck with me, as did Mom's hope and faith in what I could do. No one was going to make it easy for me, but it didn't matter. Passion, determination, and hard work were my keywords.

Mom would vehemently disagree if she knew what I had planned for my life. I feared I would disappoint her as thoroughly as Margarita had, if not more than she did, in parts because I knew how much she had sacrificed for me. She wanted me to be a doctor. Abuelo Carlos had been a native healer in Ixtepec. He was so good that even with the competition of modern medicine, his patients preferred going to him, and he helped people until the day he passed. Mom told me I would excel as a doctor, but I envisioned my future on a green field with bright lights shining down on me, kicking about a ball of synthetic leather, scoring goals to the cheers of adoring crowds.

Margarita said I would fare better as a journalist or a tortured writer, letting my pen do my talking for me. She thought all writers were social outcasts, people who had suffered some trauma in their youths, and expressed it with their pens. "Real writers," Margarita would stress, "not the ones that choke up the world now." I had no idea whether I should be pleased that she called me a real writer or annoyed at her insinuation that I was a social outcast. I chose the former, instantly forgiving Margarita. She had no tact nor filter; she said what was on her mind without restraint, sparing no one of the bluntness of her words.

The dreams they had for me were beautiful, but they weren't what I wanted. Mom always told me to fight for my ideals. My ambition was to get a position as a striker on the school's soccer team before graduating.

"What's the plan?" Fernando asked.

"I can't explain it yet. I just came up with it last night. But I wrote it down so we can both go over it at lunch," I signed.

"It'd better work," Fernando continued, his face somewhat less drawn and pale. He was regaining his composure. "I'm tired of seeing your sultry pout when the coach says no."

I grinned at Fernando as we reached school. "It'll work, trust me," I gestured at him. "I have it all figured out."

He grinned back at me then stiffened as a feminine voice cried something out. We both looked back, and we saw Seema hurrying toward us with a wide grin on her face. It suddenly became too hot; Sacramento was warm enough on most days, but it felt like someone had cranked the dial up a couple of notches. My palms were sweaty, and I had a hard time breathing.

Fernando's thin, foxlike face crumpled in a scowl of distaste.

"What does she want?" he said venomously, still angry on my behalf.

I understood what Seema had done was wrong, but I couldn't hold a grudge against her forever, though Fernando seemed like he was going to.

"Let's go," Fernando said to me, already turning. I caught hold of his hoodie to dissuade him.

"That'd be rude," I gestured.

Fernando gave a long, suffering sigh, putting on a resigned face. "Bleeding heart," he signed back at me, and I grinned widely. "I hope she doesn't use your face as a punching bag again."

Seema finally caught up with us, out of breath, her face red.

"Hi," she panted. I smelled mint on her breath. "Sorry," she said, taking a step back.

I nodded at her. Fernando grunted and cast his gaze aside; it was his way to dismiss her and express his stance of hostility. Seema edged away from him, her eyes a bit wary.

There was a moment of awkward silence, and knowing she didn't understand sign language, there was no way for me to broach a conversation. Fernando was tight-lipped. I nudged him with my elbow and rolled my eyes toward Seema. He grumbled before asking Seema in a curt tone what she wanted.

"I just wanted to apologize for the other day," she said, wringing her hands, looking directly at me. Her eyes were hazel, more green than brown, and I felt I could lose myself in them. "I shouldn't have slapped you. I overreacted, and for that, I'm really sorry. I would very much like it if we put this behind us and work towards being amicable classmates or even friends." She stopped fidgeting her fingers and settled for swinging her arms instead. A nervous tic, I guess.

Fernando seemed to have retired from responding on my behalf, so I gave Seema a nod. That seemed to satisfy her as the blinding smile came out again like the sun moving out from the cover of a dark cloud. It was a smile that demanded a similar reaction, and I smiled back at her.

"Thanks, Diego." She was almost bouncing, and her excitement was infectious. "See you in class. Bye, Fernando," she added before springing off.

Fernando sniffed in disdain and glanced at me. I hurriedly lost my soppy grin. He looked at me suspiciously for a moment and shook his head.

"Let's go," he said. "The bell will be ringing soon."

Seema sat down near us in the cafeteria. She turned around and gave a friendly wave in our direction. I waved in return, while Fernando scowled and looked away. Sebastian saw her waving at us. He shot a dark scowl in our direction before leaning close to Seema, and they exchanged furious whispers, following which Sebastian reeled back. He looked back at me again, his ears red, and his eyes burning with anger. I was amused, and there was this other light feeling I couldn't fathom. I gave Sebastian a cheery wave, and the bewildered look on his face made me smile.

In AP English class, Mr. Hoffman dozed in his chair. Sebastian took that opportunity to spit wads of paper through a straw into an unknowing classmate's hair. I showed Fernando my plan, and after going through it a couple of times, he signed that it could work, and we high-fived. Mr. Hoffman jerked awake and started a monologue about Franz Kafka's best work. It lulled even the brightest mind to sleep. While everyone else was pretending to jot down his words and stifling yawns of boredom, I was on a soccer field, dreaming of my name being chanted by thousands of adoring fans.

People always seem to have a particular look on their faces when you force them to eat their own words and agree with you or when they are about to disappoint you. Their faces tense up when they consider the best way to speak, in a way that would either save their pride or lessen the sting of rejection. When someone is planning to let you down, there will be a hint of regret and sympathy in their eyes, even if it's fabricated. But when it comes to eating their own words, what is in their eyes could best be described as agony and a bit of irritation. When that light appeared in Coach Miller's eyes, I knew I had won.

"Fine, Herrera," he said after a torturously long minute. He had finally let me on the team. I had to resist the urge to pump my fist in the air, but my impossibly wide grin must have shown my excitement as he grunted with disapproval. I had never been happier in my life.

"Practice starts tomorrow after school, Herrera. You'll meet the rest of the team then."

"Yes, Coach. I'll be there," I gestured, my hands trembling with joy.

Coach Miller grunted again. He was one of the two instructors who understood sign language. The other, Mr. Hoffman, was the only teacher who called me out to answer questions in class. While I signed out the answers, he translated it for the students with a look I could only describe as patronizing. There was a barely restrained childlike glee to him as he explained what I had signed to the others. It was almost indecent to watch, and I resented being put on display like that for him to show his skill, which the others sorely lacked.

Once, he had regaled the other teachers with the story of how he had come to learn sign language. According to him, a girl in his neighborhood was just like me. He had shot a sheepish, apologetic look my way while I stood, waiting for him to dismiss me. Mr. Hoffman claimed the poor girl was friendless, and since her parents couldn't give a hoot about her, he had taken it upon himself to befriend her. He started taking sign language classes and reading up about her disability to understand how to "relate" to her. I don't doubt he did it with good intentions, but his need for others to make mention of his gesture and applaud it baffled and irritated me. While other teachers were quite content to treat me as a slightly different student with a slightly different need, most of the time with pity and tolerance, Mr. Hoffman seemed to be stuck halfway between an object of pity and an object of fascination.

I think he was genuinely baffled by the fact that I was functioning so well in society. I wasn't handicapped by my disability. For all intents and purposes, I was a regular, hormonal 16-year-old. I guessed he didn't want me to act like the others so I could fit in the box he had prepared for me. The girl he had talked about in his tale had gone to a special-needs school. According to him, she had friends that were like her.

Maybe he expected me to be that way, too. So, he interrogated me every chance he got. I had a weird feeling Mr. Hoffman was documenting my life story somewhere, regaling his book club members about Diego Herrera, who lived a life no one expected him to live. I would give them something to talk about when I went pro like Simon Ollert.

Even though he was a consistent pain, he was the only teacher who understood my other passion, the obsessive need to read. *The need to better yourself,* he had said in that condescending manner of his, *as all human beings should.* In the six months he had been my teacher, I had read more books than I had in my entire life. He encouraged me to ask questions about what I read and seek answers beneath the layers of words.

Thankfully, no one else paid that much attention to me, so knowing I only had to deal with him made school life much more bearable. Sebastian, who poked fun at my disabilities, my race, and made stereotypical jokes about everything, was more comfortable to tolerate, even when he made it a point to read out news of illegal Mexican immigrants being deported, much to Fernando's displeasure and anger during homeroom.

I liked Coach Miller, and I would go as far as to say he was my favorite teacher, even though I had been battling for so long for him to accept me on the team. He was gruff and often abrupt, but he genuinely cared about the people under his charge and looked out for them. Sometimes I thought he was trying, in his perspective, to protect me by denying me. I respected that, but I didn't let that stop me.

"Herrera, remember what I said. One little slip and you are out!" he growled, but I didn't take it to heart.

I nodded at him. "Thanks, Coach," I signed with a smile, and as he gruffly waved me away, his face was red, but it could have been the sun.

I was practically floating when I grabbed my backpack and went off in search of Fernando to tell him the good news. He was as excited as I was and declared we celebrate a party at Antonio's. He was going to spend his pocket money on pizza. He didn't seem to have taken note that I was a probationary player, and I wasn't pushing it.

∽⌖⌁⌁⌁⌁⌁⌁⌁⌁⌁⌁⌖∽

"God, she's everywhere!"

I craned my neck towards the door, the direction Fernando was scowling in to see Seema enter Antonio's with a couple of girls. I gulped and hastily looked away before she found me staring. Although I wished I hadn't asked him to, Fernando provided enough commentary to let me know where she was.

"She's coming here with all her girl pals," he hissed, then groaned. "I swear, man, she's stalking us."

There was a warm feeling in the pit of my stomach at the thought of Seema stalking me.

"Hi," she said breathlessly but cheerily. "Are these seats taken?"

I shook my head in negation at the same time as Fernando said yes. There was a moment of awkward silence before one of Seema's friends broke it by tapping her on the shoulder and pointing to one of the free tables tucked away in a corner. Seema gave her a frown. The girl shrugged it off and directed the rest of the girls to the open table. Only Seema was left, standing awkwardly and towering over us. I tapped the table to gain Fernando's attention, and we both communicated silently using facial expressions. I won our little argument, and Fernando turned to Seema with a carefully composed expression.

"What I meant was, we were expecting someone else, but the person is running a bit late, and we aren't sure if they'll be coming again. But you can have it for now, if you want." It cost him a lot to be polite to someone he disliked.

"Thank you," Seema said, pulling out a chair and taking her seat. "Who are you expecting? If I may ask."

"Diego's sister, Margarita," Fernando said without blinking.

"I'll keep you company till she arrives. Since I just moved here, I'd love to meet her. One can't have too many friends."

Fernando was about to deliver a scathing response, so I kicked his shin under the table.

"We don't—ugh, what the heck?" he lamented.

"What's wrong?" she inquired.

"Nothing. Something bit me, I think," Fernando lied, glaring at me.

Seema giggled, covering her mouth with her hand. "You guys are such dorks."

Fernando grunted and looked away. I smiled at her, wondering why I was happy to be called a dork and why the warm feeling in my stomach kept increasing. My head was dizzy with emotion.

"Aren't you keeping your friends waiting?" Fernando asked her, gesturing toward the table where her friends were with a lift of his chin.

Seema barely glanced at them before saying she wasn't delaying them.

She spent close to half an hour at our table, directing her questions to me and having Fernando answer most of them. Halfway through the conversation, I took out my notepad so I could answer her myself, and Fernando could glower at the street through the window in peace.

"Do you want my number?" she asked me. I paused for a microsecond but then nodded yes. Not because I didn't want to say yes, but so I wouldn't appear too eager. Seema only beamed at me before scribbling her number down in sloppy handwriting.

"See you in school tomorrow, Diego, Fernando." She gave him a brief nod, which he returned with a short jerk of his head before she waved at me. I waved back, and she made her way down to her friend's table.

"Let's get out of here," Fernando said with a frown. Seema's visit had spoiled his mood.

He recovered his excellent humor once we were out of Antonio's. Soon, he was shooting questions at me about what I would do now that I was on the team and when the practice sessions were so he could come to watch me flail about on the field. I told him that I appreciated his interest in coming to see me play. He smiled.

My high spirit continued until I got home and pulled the screen door open. Mom and Margarita were in the middle of the living room, arguing their heads off. I felt my good mood rapidly spoiling, and even though they stopped at the sight of me, I couldn't conjure the feeling I had before. I forced a smile anyway.

"Diego, how was school today?" Mom asked, breathless, and with an off guard expression on her face.

"Fine, I guess. I got accepted into the soccer team," I gestured. Try as I might, the previous excitement and joy that had filled me to the brim were gone. Even Mom couldn't work up the effort to be happy for me; her eyes were dull, and her face had an expression of worry and exhaustion. Nonetheless, she forced a smile for me and told me it was fantastic news.

Margarita congratulated me in a loud, cheery tone and with a fixed smile.

"I'll be off then, Mom. See you later, Diego."

Neither of us moved to stop her as she left the house. I wondered why they had been arguing and thought it might be for the same reason. Mom had repeatedly warned Margarita not to smoke marijuana in the house, and much to her displeasure and anger, Margarita ignored her warnings. It was apparent she wanted Margarita to stop smoking, but she based her approach on yelling, then ignoring and wishing it away. Not the best method.

Sighing, Mom turned to me and enfolded me in a hug before mussing my hair.

"I'm proud of you, Diego," she said to me.

The coach had been right when he had told me that getting on the team would be more comfortable than staying on it. He was always picking on me. Once, he threatened to bench me for the rest of the season if I didn't get it together. He wanted his team to move like a well-oiled machine, a multitentacled organism that shared the same mind. Most of the players had been on the team for a year or two, so Coach Miller's way wasn't strange to them. I was new, and so was everything else. Hence, I couldn't help but feel they were bullying me, and Coach Miller was deliberately picking on me so I would get frustrated and quit the team. It wasn't the quick game in the park with other boys in my neighborhood where anything goes. The game was a taste of what professional soccer was about, and it made me all the more determined to prove I could be an essential gear in Coach Miller's machine. I was going to take his harsh words and use them as motivation.

I was a bit familiar with the boys on the team. Some were in the same classes as I was, and others I had seen around school. The first day of practice almost gave me a debilitating nervous breakdown. I came close to quitting on three different occasions, but I hadn't come that far to stop, so I continued. I was worried about how my new teammates would treat me. Would they be wary of me? Hostile? Contemptuous? Full of pity? It turned out my fears were baseless. They were a bit suspicious, but welcomed me as one of their own and tried to be sensitive to my disabilities. I got the feeling Coach Miller must have had a long talk with them before my arrival. We never became close friends, but we had the bond of being teammates in a small high school in downtown Sacramento.

The captain had been the one to explain to me that Coach Miller wasn't necessarily cruel, and it was his way of getting the best out of his team. If his constant railing made the player quit, then he wasn't meant for the team in the first place. Besides, Coach Miller was under pressure as well. Despite his fantastic game tactic, Cutler High hadn't won a soccer trophy in four years. The principal had become disillusioned with the team and issued an ultimatum: unless they won the championship this season, he would have no choice but to disband the soccer team.

He had planned not to admit a new team member so he could focus on those who were already familiar with his training routine, but I had changed his mind, and he had been forced to break his vow. Knowing that had made me respect Coach Miller even more, and I tried harder than ever not to let him down.

Being on the soccer team didn't change a thing except for giving Sebastian a new subject to use against me. When we were waiting for Ms. Perry, our AP calculus teacher, he had made a joke about how the soccer team would soon be accepting monkeys to play on the field since they had let the dumb guy in. No one but his sidekick laughed, and another member of his crew, Joshua, delivered a punchline: "At least monkeys could hear the whistle."

It took all my strength to keep Fernando from taking a swing at them, even though I would have loved nothing more than to put him in his place, but I distracted myself by trying to keep my best friend from landing in detention.

After the laughter had died down, it was Nick, the goalkeeper, who came to my defense.

"At least Diego didn't pee his pants and run away from the post squealing like a little girl before the ball could touch him. I had no idea your voice could get that high, Sebastian."

That had the entire class guffawing, except Sebastian and his cronies. Ms. Perry's entrance put a stop to the laughter. As she began her lecture, Nick turned to give me a wink.

Nick's insult temporarily halted Sebastian's thirst for my blood until a week before the first game of the season, when he and his friends came at me with a vengeance. They bombarded me with insults and jeers and offered sympathies for the supposed shots I would get to the head. There were bets on how long I'd last in the game before being hauled off the field on a stretcher.

I did my best to ignore Sebastian and his minions and stop Fernando from responding to their taunts. They weren't worth the effort or the consequences, I repeatedly told myself. Sebastian was deliberately trying to goad me into a fight so I would get kicked off the team, and I wasn't going to give him that satisfaction. I hadn't endured Coach Miller's yelling on the field and the ache that never seemed to leave my body to lose it all to a bully;

it just wasn't worth it.

The day before the game, Sebastian cornered me by my locker; his friends flanked him and effectively caged Fernando and me. In a loud voice, he said I was the product of two addicts, a hooker and a junkie—both illegal Mexicans, followed by a host of other horrific things I don't want to recount. He was on a mission to make me snap. I would have taken a swing at him, but Fernando beat me to it.

Sebastian was as surprised as I was when Fernando launched himself at him, tackling him to the ground while taking several swings. Sebastian's surprise had left enough opportunity for Fernando to get in a couple of good hits, before Sebastian recovered, returning the blows.

I dove into the fray to pull Fernando off him, earning an elbow to the face, but I latched on to him just as Sebastian's friends helped him up. Fernando's shirt was ripped and tattered, and his eyes were shooting daggers. The arrival of Principal Harris stopped him from attacking Fernando.

"What's going on here?" he demanded. Sebastian volunteered an explanation.

"It was Cortez, Principal Harris. He attacked me for no reason."

"That's a lie!" Fernando said fiercely. "He called Diego's mom an addict and a hooker!"

Principal Harris' gray eyes flicked to me. "Regardless of what he may have said," he began, his eyes slowly scanning the three of us, "fighting isn't condoned here at Cutler. Detention for both of you—two weeks of it! And after the game tomorrow night, both of you will clean the field and bleachers."

Then he turned, addressing the crowd that had gathered during the fight. "If everyone is not out of this hallway in three seconds, then all of you are going to get one week of detention as well."

The crowd dispersed. Principal Harris wasn't known for his sense of humor.

"You can let go of Cortez now, Fernando. All of you to the nurse's office so she can clean up your injuries."

"Are you all right, Herrera?" Sean, the team captain, asked me. "I heard about the fight. The skinny dude, he's your friend, right?"

I nodded yes.

"Sebastian is a jerk. He deserves all the punches he gets. Don't beat yourself up over it."

It was good advice, but I was concerned about Fernando. It wasn't like him to resort to violence, and I was worried Sebastian would retaliate. Sebastian wasn't the type to forgive and forget. And once there was no witness around, he would descend on Fernando like a hurricane with the help of his bulky friends. We were going to have to live the rest of our high school life looking over our shoulders and praying Sebastian forgot about the slight, which was very unlikely. It was also horrible that Fernando had two weeks of detention under his belt; his parents demanded nothing but the best behavior from him. He would probably be grounded, in addition to spending his time in the detention room.

"Forget about it," Fernando said to me with a scowl when I asked if he was all right. One side of his face was bruised and swollen, and he had a bandage above his left eyebrow.

I wanted to tell him how reckless he had been by rising to Sebastian's insult, but I said he had a mean punch, and it got me the response I needed. He gave a small smile that quickly faded when his split lip opened again.

"Mom's going to kill me when she hears what happened. I'm sure the principal has already called our parents. I wonder how Sebastian's mom reacted when Principal Harris called to inform her of his behavior. She would probably say something along the lines of: 'My *mijo* would never hurt a fly'", he joked, and I smiled.

"You'll be fine," I tried to assure him, but we both knew that was a lie. Mrs. Cortez might be small and sweet on a regular day, but when given the cause to, she could be like a hungry lioness on a rampage. Fernando's detention would provide her with plenty of justification.

The scowl resettled between his brows as we neared his house, and he started trembling as we approached the picket fence.

"You're completely done for, bro," I signed to him, trying to be humorous.

Fernando smiled weakly.

"I'll see you later, Diego. Pray for me." He took a deep breath and opened the front gate.

Fernando later told me that his mom didn't fly into a rage as he expected. He had only gotten the we-are-disappointed-in-you lecture before she gave him a package of frozen peas for his bruise.

My entire family showed up for the game, as well as Fernando's mom and his uncle. Fernando had told me this in the locker room as I paced, hoping my nerves would settle down. I was a bit relieved when the coach left me on the bench for the first half, but I got myself together and started warming up with restless energy. I wanted to be on the field so bad I was trembling with anticipation and frustration at Coach Miller.

The game was between our school and Golden Hills High. As I sat on the bench, I studied the tactics employed by the opposing team. They were more reckless, taking any chance to score. And score they did. A player from Golden Hills High got a yellow card, and another from theirs got a red card. Before the referee blew the half-time whistle, they had two goals in, and Jay, our striker, had a twisted ankle.

"Herrera!" Coach Miller called to me. "You're up."

It was the best night of my life. The nervousness and anxiety had melted away, and all that was left was a sense of urgency. The referee blew the whistle, and we moved.

Coach Miller had trained us to be a single unit, and we moved like one. I didn't know what changed in the second half, but our team had a renewed sense of purpose, an aura of rejuvenation. We had nothing to lose and everything to win. It all seemed like a blur, but I still remember the emotions I felt. I recalled the sting of my salty sweat as it dribbled down my forehead into my eyes. I felt the press of my fellow teammates' bodies as they lumped into a group hug after the first goal. I also remember how I'd dropped to the grass on my knees after the second goal. I was shouting at the top of my lungs after the tiebreaker. I knew I wasn't making a sound, but I'd needed an outlet for everything I was feeling. The crowd clapped and cheered at the victory.

The goal was just the beginning of what I had dreamed of experiencing all of my life: the lights, the screaming, the feeling of scoring. At that point, I could have died with a satisfied smile on my face. There was another group hug after the referee blew the whistle to signify the end of the game. I saw Mom pushing through the crowd, one of her hands holding onto Miguel's, tears running down her face. The group of people around me dispersed to let her enfold me into one of her warm, tight hugs, laughing and crying at the same time.

"That was awesome, dude!" Fernando told me. "You should have seen Sebastian's face when you scored the first goal! I have to go. Trash pickup duty. See you later, man."

I still don't see what has everyone raving about soccer," Margarita said during our ride back home.

Her words weren't enough to dampen my mood. I was still floating on cloud nine while Miguel and Margarita got into an argument over soccer.

This feeling would be the first of many.

CHAPTER 5

Mom promised to get me a car as a present for my sixteenth birthday, even though I had been sixteen for a while now. Not something fancy, just inexpensive, fuel-efficient, and only after passing my driver's test. She and Dad didn't have a car; Mom didn't see the need for it because they couldn't get driver's licenses, as they were undocumented citizens. Not even Margarita had a car, but she told me her boyfriend did have one. A 1978 Chevrolet, she said with a proud gleam in her eyes. I asked her where he had gotten the money for it. Mike was always short of cash and borrowing from her. Margarita shrugged and offered nothing else; I took the initiative and changed the subject.

Ever since she returned from wherever she'd been, Margarita had been sullen and withdrawn, punctuated by bouts of snapping at everyone before retreating further into depression. On some days, she would leave the house for long hours. Once, during one of Margarita's long walks, a friend of Mom's, Carlota, had visited and told Mom she had spotted Margarita around Cannon Industrial Park, exchanging something with some hoodlum. We all understood the implication of the bomb Carlota dropped, but Mom brushed it off as a case of mistaken identity and quickly saw Carlota out of the house. When Margarita returned, her face was pale and drawn, her lips pinched into thin, white lines. Only her eyes had color, and they were glistening fiercely. I stayed up with Mom until Margarita came home, mostly to keep her company, but also to stop their argument from escalating.

It didn't work. I would have had an easier time becoming Superman and stopping a meteorite from entering the earth's atmosphere. Neither paid attention to me as they railed at each other, making enough noise to wake the dead. I was partly scared and partly grateful no one called the cops; maybe it was because half the people on our street had something to hide, as we did.

Mom threw the vase that rested on the antique coffee table in the middle of the living room at Margarita—flowers, water, and all. She missed her by a hairs breadth; the vase exploded against our family portrait that was hanging on the wall, and everything came crashing down. Margarita stormed out of the house and into the night. When I went after her, she warned me to stay away from her before disappearing into the shadows.

I trudged back inside, saddened and frustrated I couldn't bring her back. Mom sat on the couch, her face in her hands, and shoulders shaking from sobbing. I couldn't do anything but comfort her. It was a hard night for both of us. I led her to the room she shared with Dad, who often left without saying a word. After she cried herself to sleep, I covered her and went back to the living room to clean up the product of Mom's wrath. I stayed there all night in case Margarita returned and needed someone to let her in, but she didn't.

For three days, the house was in a constant state of gloom. Miguel was perplexed, wondering why Mom was behaving as if someone had died. He kept on asking where Margarita was, why the glass on the picture frame had tape on it, and the reason the vase was missing from the coffee table. I guessed Mom blamed herself for driving Margarita off. Not knowing whether her daughter was safe was driving her out of her mind. I wanted to go down to the police station and report Margarita missing, but that would be a stupid thing to do as it would end in my family being deported back to Mexico, to the hot street in Ixtepec, where Mom sold snacks and fruit juices and dreamed of a better life.

On the third day, in the sunny afternoon, when Mom's frayed nerves were at their breaking point, Margarita waltzed in looking tired and dirty, but beautiful, and unusually chirpy. Mom embraced her, ignoring how awful she smelled, just happy she was back. I wasn't as quick to forgive, but I got my feelings across by glowering at her.

No one questioned her about where she had been for the last three days. I could see Mom wanted to, but she also wanted peace and to heal the rift between them, so she pretended the spat never occurred. Later, when I questioned Margarita as to where she'd been and what she'd been doing, she gave a mocking laugh and ruffled my hair.

"Dieguito," she said with a jeering light in her eyes. "What I've been doing would burn your naïve ears if they could hear me."

Inside, I felt my blood boiling in anger at her scorn. For the first time in my life, I wanted her gone from the family. She had always been the troublesome one, the spiteful one, and when she was gone off to God knows where, everything was very peaceful. She had only returned to rile everyone up.

Margarita seemed to have known she had crossed a line be-cause she had presented me with a pair of soccer cleats. Her rea-son was she had missed my last birthday. I wanted to remain an-gry with her, but I couldn't. They were Nike cleats and quite ex-pensive. I wanted to ask her where she'd gotten the money to buy them when she had no job, but I decided not to bring up the subject. She and Mom had already gotten into an argument because of that a week ago. Mom had told her she could work afternoon shifts at the store she worked at, but Margarita had given a scornful laugh and told her she would not slave away for a few dollars as Mom did. Mom had slapped her for that, and Margarita had taken her hours-long walk.

The cleats had been five days ago, and we had made up. Mom had informed me of her decision to buy me a car the previous night as we finished cleaning up after dinner. She had finally saved enough to buy one, and if I passed my driving test, I would get the car I wanted, providing she could afford it. I hugged her tight, expressing all the words I wanted to say with that timeless gesture. She understood me well and mussed my hair.

"You'll do very well, my Dieguito. You'll see," she promised.

I went to the local library to borrow a book on driving for beginners. I stayed up at night reading it under my covers with my phone's flashlight.

Margarita found me with the book the next morning, and she pried it out of my hands, which woke me up. I sat up while she looked through it with a stern expression on her face.

"Dieguito, only you would go to a library when everyone else uses the internet." She tossed the book back on my bed before flopping down beside me, drawing her knees up to her chin and circling her ankles with her arms, a thoughtful expression on her face. I left her to her thoughts while I hunted for a charger for my dead phone.

"Mom is buying you a car, isn't she?" she turned to me. I nodded, and a flash of deep dislike and resentment appeared in her eyes, but it was gone in an instant, replaced with a smile.

"What are you going to tell her to buy? Or are you leaving it up to her? You might end up with Gustavo's beat-up Cavalier if you do!"

I didn't respond to her. Gustavo was one of Dad's friends who lived a block away from our place. I didn't like much about him, but I liked his Cavalier. I thought it looked decent, and with a fresh coat of paint, it would look even more so. It was then we began having a conversation about cars, though Margarita did most of the talking while I inputted once in a while. She was quite talkative when given a chance to be, and I was glad she was communicating again, instead of her prolonged sullenness that made it difficult to approach her. It was then Margarita mentioned the Chevrolet and how she and Mike had taken great pleasure and pride in it. She had driven it once or twice, fast through the streets, and had the cops after them, but they had thankfully escaped.

I listened with burgeoning horror at how she had a narrow escape from the law. How could she have been so reckless? But then again, that was who she was. Margarita had always lived her life her way regardless of what others had to say about it. Still, I was glad she wasn't at home that often. Miguel was at that impressionable age, and the strained relationship between Mom and Dad upset him, but he found solace in soccer, his friends, and video games. He lived in awe for action and the antihero protagonists in movies who thumb their noses at the law. He would be utterly mesmerized if Margarita told him the story of her close brush with the authorities.

I was worried about her. Apart from her skinniness and the unhealthy pallor to her skin, I got the feeling she was sad and badly in need of help, but she was as prickly as a thorn and wouldn't let anyone come near her defenses. Each time I brought the subject of her well-being up, she would either brush it aside or give me a curt answer before switching the topic or yelling at me, telling me to keep my nose out of her business before storming off. I knew it would be no use telling Mom to talk to her while they were both on edge and taking care not to offend one another. Dad was too distant from our lives for me to approach him to talk to Margarita, and Miguel was too young.

"He wanted a Porsche or something else just as flashy, but I convinced him to go for something cool and classy. I have an auto magazine with me," she commented as she hunted through the duffel bag she had brought with her. It was the very duffel bag she had expressly forbidden Miguel and me to go through. I wondered where Mike could have gotten enough money to want to buy a Porsche, and the answer came to me immediately.

Margarita found the catalog and came back to me. We spent a while flipping through the glossy pages and looking at cars. I wanted to do something else, like finish reading my book and texting Fernando. I already knew I wanted the beat-up Cavalier she had scornfully dismissed, but I invented enthusiasm because I thought she needed this.

"Cool, now you'll be able to drive me everywhere!" Fernando exclaimed. He was even more excited than I was, listing all the places we would go. I told him okay as long as he paid for the gas. That had dented his enthusiasm a bit, but not for long.

"Good things are coming your way, amigo. First, you got onto the soccer team, then you won your first game, and now you're getting a new car. I wish I had your luck."

I tried not to preen at his words, but I wasn't going to deny they made me feel good. Maybe it was partly luck, but I had worked hard to make the team and even harder to remain on it. Winning that game had been the culmination of all my efforts. The car was the icing on the cake.

"Have you thought about the college you want to go to?" Fernando asked. "I've written a bunch of application letters to colleges out of state. I need to get away from Sacramento."

I had no answer for him, so I shrugged, concentrating on my milkshake. Mom wanted me to go to a local college so I could come home every weekend. She told me she couldn't bear to be away from me for long. I was her Dieguito, her little Diego.

Fernando thought nothing of my silence and continued talking. "My birthday is coming up. Do you have any plans that day?"

I gave him a sly look and held my index finger to mime a motion of padlocking my lips and tossing the phantom key away. It was difficult to believe he would be eighteen in a few days. I had skipped another grade when I was fifteen, so even though he was older than I was, we were both seniors. While I looked my age and sometimes older, Fernando looked like he would be between thirteen and fifteen, and people often treated him like a child even though he was older than me.

"How about loaning me your car?" he suggested. I must have had a worried look on my face, as he hurriedly went on. "Just for a day."

"So you can wreck it?" I signed.

Fernando looked hurt. "I see I'm not trusted. Fine then, you can be my chauffeur for that day, drive me everywhere, and still pay for the gas."

I shrugged. "But you're paying for the milkshakes," I reminded him.

He gave a theatrical groan.

"And we're meeting your uncle after," I added.

Fernando's uncle, Guillermo, was giving me private driving lessons. Unlike Fernando and his parents, he had entered the United States legally and owned a convenience store near Granite Regional Park, where Fernando worked part-time. He had taken a liking to me and sometimes gave both of us money we either spent on pizza or split to save. We chose to keep it most of the time.

I was supposed to meet him by five when Fernando returned to work. Guillermo was built thin like Fernando and wore horn-rimmed glasses. He spoke to me in Spanish most of the time, but he spoke so fast I was sure even a person who didn't need a hearing aid would have a difficult time following. I drove us around downtown Sacramento, mostly going through the back streets where there were fewer cars. I made sure I followed the proper protocols with Guillermo nodding approvingly at my choices.

"We'll meet again tomorrow for another lesson, even though I think you don't need it. Send my greetings to your Mom and Dad," he said to me after dropping me off at my doorstep. With a friendly bye, he drove off.

We met five more times for additional lessons. At the end of each session, he would insist I return for another just for certainty, and after six training sessions, he was confident in my driving ability.

"*Muy bien.* Now you'll ace that test," he assured me.

I had a difficult time sleeping the night before the test due to my nervousness. I recited the rules and protocols to driving safely to reassure myself I had everything down pat. I couldn't stop myself from imagining the way things could go wrong. I finally fell asleep shortly before dawn, my eyes unable to keep themselves open. It felt like I had just closed my eyes when I was shaken awake by Mom.

The written exam was straightforward. The actual driving test was what had my stomach in knots. I almost quit and went home, but I didn't. My examiner was strict, and the way she held her clipboard was menacing to me. She began by informing me she was aware of my disabilities but was not going to cut me any slack because of it. It irritated me that she would think that way. The flash of anger burned away some of my nervousness, although my palms were still damp with sweat.

I thought everything went smoothly, but I couldn't be so sure of her expression. I drove us back to the center and then awaited the verdict.

"Well, Diego Herrera, you passed your driver's test. Congratulations."

Mom made tamales that night to celebrate. And after peppering my face with kisses, she told me we would go to Gustavo's to purchase his Cavalier.

"Told you so," Margarita said.

I shrugged. I didn't mind the Cavalier in the least. I didn't know how much Mom had paid for the car, but I knew she had made a great effort to be able to buy it, and I appreciated it.

"Too bad it didn't come with a giant bow," Margarita remarked, leaning on the porch railing when the car pulled up.

Her words didn't hurt me because I had a car and she didn't. Despite how old it was, I liked it; more importantly, the mileage was still good.

CHAPTER 6

"Sean is having a party at his house tonight, wanna come?" Nick asked me, hitching up his backpack.

That he approached me was shocking, but what he'd asked was even more so. It took some time for his words to sink in, and when they did, my eyes widened. A party! I had never been invited to one before, except for Jeremy's Bar Mitzvah across the street that Miguel and I went to, as well as Fernando's birthday parties. Sometimes, I heard noises from three doors down, always so loud that I could hear them even without my hearing aids.

Margarita had gone to her fair share of parties when she was in high school. She was pretty popular back then before she ditched all her friends and took on with some unsavory characters. Back then, her friends threw parties almost every weekend, and Margarita went to all of them. It distressed her if she missed one or didn't have a new dress to wear. Mom couldn't afford to buy Margarita dresses every month, let alone every weekend. And after they had an argument in which she accused Mom of pinching pennies, she had found a way to get herself new clothes: shoplifting. It had provided her with the clothes that Mom couldn't afford to buy her, besides makeup, sunglasses, and other things.

It horrified me that she was stealing. But Margarita was flippant about her crime, shrugging and claiming every other girl did it. I had tried to stress the fact that if she kept up with it, she would get caught. If they called the cops, she would get herself, and our parents discovered and deported. It didn't seem to stop her, though, and she never got caught. Sometimes, it seemed she only cared about herself and her needs—no one else's. This made me upset. What on earth would our family do if they were deported back to Mexico? The United States was the only country I had ever known. How could she be so selfish?

She still went partying now and then. She'd sneak out of the house to attend. She'd get drunk or high, and return home where I'd be waiting to let her in through the window. Most times, I would hold her hair back while she puked her guts out into a bucket. The partying spiked during her senior year. She was at parties three times a week, even on school nights, and left me to cover for her. When she got into college, everything mercifully stopped, and I felt like I could breathe again.

The depiction of those parties in movies and the way Margarita had let herself run wild at the expense of her education put me off the whole idea of partying. Our family lived by the doctrine of keeping our heads down and not doing anything to attract untoward attention.

Fernando wasn't keen on the idea of parties either. Police often busted the teenagers' parties, and the last thing he or his family members would want was him in custody. Since it wasn't our scene, we spent our Saturday nights playing checkers or cards with his uncle. We lost to him most of the time and had to write an IOU that no one took seriously. Uncle Guillermo often told us he was using the rules of the games to teach us about life. Luck and strategy were all that mattered, according to him.

Before Nick approached me about the party on Saturday, my plan had been poker night with Uncle Guillermo and Fernando and a sleepover at their place. When I had gotten over the surprise of him asking me to the party, I began to consider it. I didn't think there was any harm in seeing how it was. I wouldn't touch any liquor at all.

Fernando's birthday was three days ago, and they had thrown a small party in their living room with a little cake. His dad had gifted him a case of beer with a hearty thump on his back even though the legal drinking age was twenty-one, while his uncle had given him a camera so he could actively pursue his hobby as a photojournalist. It wasn't just a hobby to him, though; Fernando wanted to pursue it as a career, but his parents were hoping he would study law.

Fernando had broken open the case of beer as we sat on a foldable deck chair in their tiny backyard.

"Doesn't taste that bad or that good either," he informed me. "I'd often wondered what made people like beer."

"Acquired taste," I signed. I was just a bit curious as to how it tasted but hadn't asked, focusing on how my lemonade tasted instead.

Maybe Fernando could come with me.

"You don't have to come if you don't want to, but the entire team will be there, and I thought you might like to come and have a fun time, especially in light of our recent victory. You can bring your friend too. Think about it."

A few days later, when I saw Fernando again, he said no as I had supposed he would.

"No!" he repeated with vehemence, shaking his head for emphasis. "That's a cop magnet, dude. We don't do cop magnet; at least I thought we didn't. Why are you betraying our solemn vows, dude?"

I raised my eyebrow at him. There had been no solemn vows, and there was no guarantee the cops were going to show up at the party.

"Four out of five parties get busted, which makes it highly likely this party you want to drag us to will also."

"On the other hand, it might be the one that doesn't," I signed.

"What's your guarantee it won't?" Fernando demanded.

"What's your guarantee it will?" I shot back at him.

He had no answer for that.

"Look, Nick told me the entire team is going, and I want them to accept me as one of them."

"They'd understand if you said you got sick."

I glowered at him until he said sorry and stopped talking. "We'll just go in and look around, have some punch, make our excuses, and leave."

"How early?" Fernando grudgingly asked.

I concealed my victorious grin. "The party starts at seven. We arrive at eight and leave by nine or ten."

"Make it nine, and we'll go to this dumb party. It might just be the one the police decide to shut down."

I didn't tell Mom I was going to a party. She assumed I'd be with Fernando, and I did nothing to correct her assumption. I felt quite ill at ease over not telling Mom the truth about our plans to go to a party. As Saturday drew closer, I wondered if Margarita ever felt this guilty when she went out to parties without Mom's knowledge. I almost told Mom about my plans for Saturday but stopped right before I confessed. It was as if it would diminish the experience if I told her. She might forbid me from going, but somehow, I doubt she would if she learned Fernando would be with me.

Fernando didn't tell his parents or uncle; they would have grounded him for the rest of life if he had been careless enough to drop a hint that he would be going on such a risky venture. The tense expression he had at school throughout the week made me think he was going to bail on me. Although I wanted to experience a high school party at least once before I graduated, I knew I didn't want to face it without Fernando. If he backed out of the plan, I would be spending my Saturday night at a quiet poker game with him and his uncle.

To my surprise, he didn't. On Saturday evening, I got ready for the party and said bye to Mom and Miguel. Margarita had done her disappearing act yet again, and we couldn't find her.

"Say hi to Fernando and Rosario for me," Mom said to me.

"I will," I signed, keeping the pleasant smile on my face, though inside, I felt sick with guilt.

Fernando's face was a mirror of mine when I got to his house. He was already waiting for me at the door, and hurriedly got into the car. Sweat trickled down his forehead. He finally starting speaking once we were a couple of blocks away from his place.

"I don't feel good about this, dude. Mom was asking questions. The last thing we need is her calling your mom to ask if I'm at your place."

"It's okay if you want to ditch." I tapped my fingers against the steering wheel.

"Nah, we're too far gone."

Sean's house, where the party was taking place, was in Midtown. It took us a few minutes to get there. Fernando whistled when we pulled into the driveway.

"Rich boy," he said to me.

I didn't respond, turning off the engine and getting out. My heart had found itself lodged in my throat again. Fernando seemed to be handling his nervousness better than I was. As he walked beside me, his face was resigned and partly curious. We walked up to the door, and I pressed on the buzzer. The door swung open a moment later, revealing Nick's beaming face.

"Diego, you came!" He seemed genuinely pleased to see me. "And Fernando, am I right?"

"Yeah, I hope you don't mind me being here."

"Of course not! Come in, guys." He ushered us into Sean's wide and marbled foyer. "They're all in the den. Hey, guys, Diego and Fernando are here!"

I felt glad that they'd warmly welcomed us. Sean was an African American boy with big, expressive eyes, and he was continually smiling.

"*Mi casa es su casa.* Sit anywhere you want," he said to Fernando and me.

"The party is just picking up. It's just us and a couple of other guys. No girls yet," he said with an apologetic expression on his face.

"Figured that might happen. Girls and makeup, am I right?"

I shrugged, feeling the knots in my stomach loosen a bit. If we left before everyone else arrived, I would consider the night a huge success.

It didn't happen that way. At first, it was awkward—Fernando and I sitting together on the couch, feeling deeply uncomfortable while we listened to the cronies as they conversed about topics that weren't familiar to us. Nick served me a drink in a red plastic cup. When he saw the reluctance on my face, he laughed.

"Relax, it's just root beer. We wouldn't dare give alcohol to a minor."

I flushed, even though I knew he'd been joking.

"Here you go, dude," he said to Fernando as he handed him a glass of root beer.

"Thanks, man," said Fernando.

I think it was after the root beer that I started loosening up. The talk diverted to familiar ground, and everyone tossed questions my way. There were mostly questions that demanded a yes or a no, universal gestures. When the answers were unusually long, Fernando interpreted for me, even though I wished I were able to myself. It didn't matter that our communication methods were limited; they included me in the conversation, and Fernando wasn't left out either. Even when others started arriving, Fernando and I remained part of the conversation.

It was when I was on my third root beer that Fernando began signaling me that we should leave. I might have relaxed and forgotten about my promise that we would go before it got late, but Fernando certainly had not.

"That must be the pizza," Sean said at the sound of the doorbell, heading towards the door. Moments later, he returned with boxes of pizza, Seema in tow. While others cheered at the sight of food, I was busy trying to stop my heart from breaking out of my ribcage. The room felt particularly hot, or maybe it was just me. My mouth was dry. I gulped down my root beer, almost choking on it.

Fernando shot me a look full of annoyance for not getting up to leave right at that moment. I immediately looked back at him with large eyes, and he mercifully left me alone.

Seema bounced over to us. "Hi, Diego, Fernando." She took a seat right next to me, and I could feel her warmth and smell the scent of vanilla emanating from her hair. It smelled so lovely.

"It's a surprise seeing you here. I didn't think parties were your scene," she said through a smile.

"Because he's deaf?" Fernando hissed at her, and her smile drooped a bit, a frown furrowing her brow.

"No, because he looks studious. I figured his way of unwinding would be a library or something. Why would you even think that?"

"Hmmm, I don't know, because you're notorious for jumping to conclusions."

I was half afraid that a scene was going to break out, but fortunately, it didn't.

"Pot, kettle," Seema said in an even voice, and Fernando looked away without another word. She smirked in victory and was about to say something to me when Nathan's voice broke in.

"Stop your suspicious whispering over there before we finish the pizza by ourselves."

Seema did most of the talking. I was content to sit, eat my pizza, and watch her speak to me. Everything else, including Fernando's warning glance, faded to the background. She said she was glad Sean invited me to his party. She inquired why I hadn't texted her yet. Before I could bring out my notepad, she was telling me this was the fifth party Sean had thrown this semester, and she had been to every single one.

"The sky is clear tonight, and the stars are shining. Do you want to go outside and take a look?"

I had barely gotten my nod out before she seized my hand and proceeded in dragging me out. I looked back to see Fernando's disapproving face before the others swarmed him. As soon as we went out the back door, Seema released my hand and flopped down on the grass. Her arms folded behind her head to serve as a pillow. I sat cross-legged next to her and looked up at the stars.

Seema had lied. There were no stars, only the moon and wispy clouds. She had a mischievous grin on her face.

"I lied," she mouthed, still smiling, and I felt an answering grin turning up the corners of my mouth.

"It's crowded inside, and I wanted you all to myself without Fernando glowering at us. What's his deal?"

I shrugged. Fernando was not quick to forgive and forget. But I didn't want to talk about Fernando. My heart was attempting to escape from my chest again, and my palms were sweaty.

Suddenly, she sat up, almost startling me. Her face was so close I could see her dimples as she smiled. Her eyes roamed over my face as I did my best not to do anything wrong to ruin our close encounter.

"Were you born this way?" she finally asked. I nodded, and her expression softened. "I'm sorry. It must be hard for you."

I shrugged. Sometimes it was, sometimes it wasn't.

"I started learning sign language," she told me, her eyes shining brightly. I felt my breath quicken as a euphoric feeling wrapped me in its shawl. "Thought I needed a hobby other than slapping random strangers," she said with a grin.

I smiled at her attempt at a joke and gestured to her that it was funny. She frowned down at my moving fingers.

"I'm still a beginner, so you'll have to slow down."

I repeated the gesture, this time slower as she stared intently at my fingers, trying to puzzle out what I was saying. She finally figured it out and smiled at me.

"Thank you." She tucked a lock of hair behind her ear, still smiling. "That's my dream… to be a comedian."

I gestured to her again, taking the time to sign out each word, telling her it was a cool dream. That earned me another smile.

"You're a cool guy, Diego," she told me, inching closer until our faces were almost touching. "A really cool guy," she said again, and then she kissed me.

Her lips were soft and warm on mine, and the shock made me forget how to breathe. It took me a second or two to recover, and I kissed her back. We stayed that way for a while, kissing, until I remembered Fernando. I broke the kiss, and she opened her eyes, looking at me with a frown of concern.

"What's wrong?" she asked in a loud voice.

I shook my head to tell her there was nothing wrong and stood up, brushing the dirt from my jeans. It had been unfair I had dragged Fernando all the way to a party he hadn't wanted to come to and then abandoned him to the mercy of strangers. I wouldn't be surprised if he had left in annoyance, but he wouldn't do that.

I helped Seema to her feet, her face worried and distraught.

"Is something wrong, Diego? Was it the kiss?"

I kissed her again, a quick press of the lips to show it wasn't because of that and slowly signed I had to go because I had promised I would help my mom with something.

That was my second lie this week, but I felt it was necessary. Seema wouldn't take kindly to being ditched in favor of Fernando, and I couldn't explain why because it would take time, and frankly, it wasn't my story to tell.

"Text me," she said, and I nodded. "You go. I'll stay here for a while longer."

I found Fernando playing beer pong with a tall guy who hadn't been there when Seema and I had left. Fernando was winning and had drunk up to six cups of beer, judging by the empty cups littering the table beside him. I was suddenly glad I was the one driving.

"Let's get out of here," he said to me after he had freed himself from his adoring fans after he won, reeking of beer with a strange light in his eyes. I thought he would be affected by all the alcohol he'd imbibed, but he looked steady on his feet.

We said bye to Nick and Sean. We got into my car and drove to Fernando's house. Knowing his parents would be asleep, we decided we would sneak into the house without anyone knowing since he had the key to the front door. We succeeded. Fernando fell asleep the instant his head hit the pillow. It took longer for me. All I could think about was Seema and the two kisses we had shared. She was still on my mind as I fell asleep with a wide grin on my face.

CHAPTER 7

"So, who are you inviting to prom?" Fernando asked me, as the bell rang and we stuffed notes into our backpacks. "It's going to be Seema, right? I don't like her." Fernando grimaced, twitching his lips in apparent disgust.

"Well, I don't like Gordo," I signed in retort, referring to the bad-tempered, three-legged cat Fernando had as a pet. I had no problem with animals at all. I even left bowls of milk out for the stray cat that often prowled the window of my small bedroom.

But Fernando's pet was a monster, and he became more of one after he got neutered. I think the little *diablo* knew how I felt about him and reciprocated accordingly, hissing whenever I came within a foot of him. Knowing of our mutual dislike, Fernando let Gordo stray out of the house whenever I was coming over, an arrangement that made me happy.

"Gordo is an angel," Fernando protested. "He just needs someone to understand him and see beneath his tough exterior."

I tried not to roll my eyes. "Gordo is just mean, plain and simple. No depth to that."

"I wouldn't expect you to understand," he shot at me. "You don't understand the bond between a man and his pet."

"And I wouldn't expect you to understand a relationship between a man and his girlfriend seeing how your beloved cat starts hissing and spitting whenever a girl gets within a mile of you."

Fernando gave me a sly grin that made me wish I hadn't signed the word girlfriend to qualify Seema. I'd just given him an avenue to tease me for the entire week, and even more, I had attributed a label to something that still was not defined.

"Girlfriend, huh?" Fernando said, a teasing light in his eyes. I rolled mine in response.

"A girl who is my friend," I tried to explain, but he wasn't buying it.

"I see. Well, I'm sure what you share with your, uh—girlfriend—isn't the same as what I share with my cat."

I let that slide as I wondered what the relationship was between Seema and me. We had never even been on a date together, and we had just kissed. Did two kisses automatically make us boyfriend and girlfriend? I was pretty sure we were friends already, maybe a bit more than just acquaintances. We hung out a couple of times after school. She waited for me at the bleachers until I was through with soccer practice, and I drove her home. Most times, we sat side by side until it was dark, and I was no longer able to read her lips, and she could no longer understand what I had written down.

Technically, she had asked me out on a date... or had at least broached the subject. She had begun by talking about the new movie that would be premiering Saturday at the local movie theater and went on and on about it. I acted on impulse and wrote on the notepad, asking her if she would like to see it with me.

I immediately wished I hadn't done that, but her face immediately lit up. She said she would love to. She had begun to learn sign language through an ASL course she was taking online to be able to communicate with me better, something I greatly appreciated. Since she was still slow at understanding the signs, I continued to use writing.

After dropping her off at her house, I drove straight to Fernando's to ask for advice and waited with extreme patience for him to stop laughing. He hugged his yowling diablo and proceeded to lay down a set of complex and complicated rules that almost made me text Seema to tell her I couldn't make it.

When I told Mom about the date, tears filled her eyes over her little Diego finally having a girlfriend. My ears burned while I tried to set her right by protesting that Seema wasn't my girlfriend. She was so lost in her excitement that she didn't even listen to my corrections. She had advice for me like Fernando had, the dos and don'ts of a first date, and reminisced about the time when Dad had first asked her out.

"He was so nervous that evening and afraid of my papa, your Abuelo. He was a bit shorter than me then. Years later, he grew some more, but back then, he had been a skinny, timid kid, a klutz," she told me with a small smile on her face.

"Papa was cleaning his carving knife when he knocked on the door, and he answered it still holding the knife. Shocked at seeing a knife in his hand, Alejandro nearly fainted. To make matters worse, papa was tall, like a giant. I know you'll be tall like him.

"He told me later Alejandro's courage had almost failed him at the sight of the knife, but he didn't tuck tail and run away; he stood his ground. Papa thought he was going to stand with me for the rest of our lives."

"I doubt Seema's dad will welcome me with a knife," I gestured, but I was doubtful. Seema lived in a tough neighborhood in downtown Sacramento, making our block seem like Elysium in comparison. Her dad owned a small butcher shop in an even worse part of town, and she was always telling me about the extreme security measures they followed. She didn't mention whether they had ever been robbed, but I had no doubt he could defend himself and his business in case of a break-in or robbery.

Mom was equally excited about Margarita's first date about five years ago. But her excitement had been punctuated by worry, and she kept giving her advice up until the moment she saw Margarita and her date outside and into the car, yelling out to her that she stay safe.

After they were gone, Mom had paced around the living room, watching the hours tick by until it was time for Margarita to return. There were no such warnings for me. It was pure excitement and the need to giggle and tell stories of past dates and pick out my clothes. Margarita had been equally full of advice, and she had told me to be calm and attentive to her needs. She said girls like guys who have an aura of mystery. I had raised my eyebrow at her, wondering how in the heck I was supposed to achieve that.

"Oh! And don't wear a suit on your first date, it makes it seem like you're trying too hard. You're just going to the movies. Wear something cool and casual, not the usual gray hoodie you wear to school that makes you look like a hoodlum."

I felt insulted by that comparison of my hoodie—not that I was planning to wear the hoodie or the suit. The suit was my Dad's, and even though Mom had used a needle and thread to tailor it to my size, it still appeared old and shabby. I had already picked out my clothes: a pair of jeans, a t-shirt, and sneakers.

"Don't forget to buy her flowers. Roses are an all-time favorite," Margarita added. "If all goes well, she might let you have your first kiss with her."

I kept my composure, careful not to let the flush that was about to manifest show on my face. If Margarita learned that I had not only my first, but also my second, third, and fourth kiss with Seema, she might faint from laughter before proceeding to tease me. Fernando had done just that when I'd told him Seema had kissed me that night at Sean's party when we were in the backyard alone, and I had kissed her again just before I came in for him. He cackled until his stomach hurt and curled himself into a ball, gasping for air while simultaneously howling with laughter.

"I'm really sorry, bro. But don't worry… next time, I won't follow you when you go to a party. Your moonlight romance won't be interrupted because of me."

I aimed a swipe at him, but he avoided it easily before dissolving into another irritating bout of laughter.

Seema had kissed me again one evening after soccer practice. Fernando had to leave earlier to get to work on time, and Seema had stayed behind, cheering at me from the bleachers. Coach Miller blew the whistle and ended the practice for the day, and I jogged to where she was. Our second game of the season had taken place the night before, and we narrowly won after a string of foolish missteps. After Coach Miller scolded us for our mistakes, we began work on a new set of tactics. The ache in my body melted away at the sight of her, and I grinned.

"Hello," I signed, breathing heavily.

"Hi," she signed back, looking up from her AP Calculus textbook. "We need to do something about Coach Miller." She pointed the butt of her pen in the direction of where he was standing. "He's more of a drill sergeant than a coach."

"Aren't they the same thing?" I signed, taking it slow, so it would be easier for her to understand.

Seema gave me a look that said I was obtuse. "One prepares soldiers for war, and the other is supposed to prepare a group of boys for a game, not a life or death situation."

"Same thing," I answered her.

She shook her head before flipping another page of her textbook and frowning at the formulas. "Hey, could you help me with this? I don't understand any of it."

I was pleased to do that. I was about to start explaining when Seema kissed me, and I leaned into the kiss.

"Thanks, Diego," she murmured against my lips as she broke off the kiss. "I understand it quite well now," she said with a wink. Her ploy had delivered fruit.

She kissed me again when I dropped her off. This time, it was a lingering kiss. It was when her elbow jabbed the horn that we sprang apart, breathless and grinning like fools. She had kissed me one last time before bounding out of the car to go into her house, and she blew a kiss at me before she closed the front door behind her.

I didn't tell Fernando about the subsequent kisses, but I knew he'd guessed from the small smile that I wore as I helped him with his work.

On the night of my date, Mom had attacked my mop of unruly hair with a wet comb to make it lie flat, but it had defeated her, and I had to spend precious minutes toweling my hair dry.

"Should I lend you my hairdryer?" Margarita teased, but I ignored her. "Dieguito, all grown up," she later commented as Mom fussed over me before I stepped out the door. "Leave him, Mama. You aren't sending him off to war; he'll come back tonight. Don't forget you need to be home by bedtime, at eleven, sharp," she called as I closed the front gate.

Seema's dad didn't greet me with any knife when he opened the door, but he wore a bloodstained apron that read "Bali's Butcher Shop." He had been friendly enough, but I had gotten the feeling he had been putting on an act for Seema's sake. There had been a tightness to his eyes that told me he didn't approve of me. I didn't want to know why.

Seema's mom was small and birdlike, and her welcome was warm and sincere. She took the flowers from me and lovingly arranged them in the vase on the mantle, then served me a cup of chai tea and told me to be patient, Seema would be out soon.

Seema had two older brothers. One was in college, and the other was at work. She told me they were tough on the exterior but soft and mushy on the inside, like her dad. I was glad about their absence, as I wasn't sure whether I could handle three people being passively hostile with me.

I had to sit in their living room for almost an hour while Seema finished getting ready. Her dad sat there, glaring at me. Her mom buzzed about, busily preparing dinner. She occasionally came to ask if I was okay, at which I nodded yes. At one point, when it had felt Seema wouldn't be coming out for a while longer, I gestured to her mother that I wanted to help her with preparing dinner, but she waved away my offer with a kind smile, telling her husband what a nice boy I was.

"Don't you think so, Bali?"

He grunted in response.

When it felt like I'd been there forever, Seema made her appearance, and my state of nerves melted away the moment I saw her. She was breathtaking in her simple, above-the-knee black dress, nothing too scandalous for her Dad, and the barely-there make up accentuated her beautiful face even more; but it was the sparkling light in her hazel eyes that made her stunning.

I stood up at the sight of her and gave her the single rose I held back from the bouquet I had offered her mom. She smiled as she received it, and then proceeded in breaking off its thorns as her mother gushed about how beautiful she was, before tucking it behind her ear.

"You should get going now." Her mom ushered us out, pressing a coat into Seema's hands. "It's cold outside. Have fun and take care."

"Young man, my daughter is to return home by ten-thirty, not a second later," her dad said, his stance full of the threat of retribution if I failed this simple task. I nodded in understanding.

"Papa," Seema protested, but she was hushed.

Our first date went quite well. We left the movie halfway because it turned out to be a comedy laced with scenes that Seema had found especially funny. She was laughing so loud that the usher had come around to warn us twice. When Seema's laughter reached a particularly loud crescendo, we let ourselves out before the usher could come around a third time.

I left my car in the movie theater's parking lot when Seema suggested we walk. We strolled around and bought samosas with mint chutney from a food truck. The stars had been out that night, and Seema hadn't been lying when she said she loved stars. She soon began pointing out constellations to me. The park had been too dark for me to read her lips, or to see signs our fingers made, and we reenacted our little romantic scene under the stars. She kept giggling as we sat side by side on the bleachers, her fingers threading through my hair and placing my hand on her knees.

After a series of little kisses and more giggling from her, we wandered back to the parking lot. My head was practically in the clouds. I drove her back to her house with thirty minutes to spare before her curfew, kissing her goodnight before driving home to be greeted by an excitable Mom who wanted to hear every minute detail.

"We only saw the movie and took a walk in the park, Mom," I explained, trying to fend off other questions.

"So, did she kiss you? Or did you kiss her?" Margarita asked from her perch on the cane chair in the corner of the living room.

I ignored her, trying and failing to stop the flush from creeping up my neck to my cheeks.

"It's none of your concern what Diego did with his girlfriend, Margarita," Mom said in my defense.

"Defending your little baby boy—"

"Margarita!" Mom shouted indignantly.

"I'm just joking, Mom," Margarita said.

"I'm joking, Diego. It's none of my business."

Her tone of voice indicated that she hadn't been joking, but in my fog of happiness, I shrugged it off. When I was finally released to go to my room, I found Seema had texted me, and with a grin on my face, I texted her back. We were still texting when Margarita came in with her knowing smile. I wondered what kind of snide comments she would have for me now, but she didn't say anything. It had been sometime around 3 a.m. when Seema and I finally said goodnight, and I had gone to bed feeling like life was a dream.

Fernando had come over the next morning and asked how the date had gone. I told him about it, leaving out the part about the make out in the park.

"Her dad sounds like he would turn you into minced meat!"

"I know."

"So, you and Seema, huh? Are you guys an item now?"

I shrugged, not wanting to put a label on something without really knowing. She might just be enjoying the time we spent together without the commitment of a boyfriend-girlfriend relationship. I wondered whether I had to ask her to be my girlfriend officially since we had gone out on a date and kissed a couple of times. I didn't want to ask her and have her look at me as if I was an idiot. Labels didn't matter to me anyway. What was important was that we were together.

CHAPTER 8

It was official now. Seema was my girlfriend. It took her a few weeks to decide we were an item. She introduced me to a friend of hers as her boyfriend, and I guessed that officially stamped our status as a couple. It had felt like I was floating in the clouds, a balloon of happiness swelling inside me. I had to formally invite her to prom after she'd lectured me that it wasn't proper to assume she would automatically go with me because we were a couple. "It's prom," she stressed. "You have to ask me out."

I did, and she squealed as if it was a surprise before saying yes. I had to depend on my sister for inputs on dates while my sarcastic friend randomly tossed spokes in her wheel to frustrate her.

"You have to rent a limo for prom. Girls expect that sort of thing. A limo, a corsage, a bouquet, and a box of chocolates if you want to do it properly," Margarita told me.

"Why?" Fernando demanded. "It isn't secretly Valentine's Day, is it?"

Margarita pierced him with a scornful look while I sat between them, trying not to appear amused. It was a week until prom, and both of them were helping me prepare for the day. Fernando was ditching prom since he had no date. According to him, the idea and tradition didn't make sense at all. He would be spending prom night operating the counter at his uncle's store, but his distaste for prom didn't stop him from giving ridiculous advice.

Fernando continued. "You do realize Diego is a broke dude and has no job, right? He'll break the bank trying to rent a limo. What's wrong with his Cavalier?"

That wasn't entirely true. I still had some savings left after paying for my suit rental. It would be enough to rent a limo for the night, buy a corsage and maybe the bouquet and chocolates, but the idea of spending so much for just one night seemed frivolous. I had to agree with Fernando on that count—what was wrong with my Cavalier? As for not having a job, that had been due to Mom's overprotectiveness, and I planned to get a part-time job when I got to college.

"She'll probably break up with you when she sees how thrifty you are. I'd encourage her to break up with my stingy brother."

"At least then he wouldn't have to sell one of his kidneys to rent a limo," Fernando shot back, and they glared at each other. Margarita relented first.

"What dress is she wearing?" she asked me.

I shrugged. "Does it matter?" I signed.

"Of course, numbskull, so you can match."

Fernando burst into a mocking laugh. "Diego is wearing a black suit. I'm sure Seema can find a black dress to match him."

Margarita gave him the stink eye. "If you aren't going to be of useful help…" she began in a growling tone.

"But I am. I'm humorously diffusing the tension. But honestly, Margarita, that doesn't make sense."

"Guys are always clueless about everything."

"Yay for feminism," Fernando signed to me, and I stifled a

smile. I didn't want to get Margarita angry when she was taking out of her precious time to help me.

"What if she's wearing purple?" Fernando asked. "Does that mean Diego would have to wear purple also? He isn't exactly the artist that was formerly known as Prince."

Margarita's glower could level cities, but Fernando met it with an innocent expression. We all knew he was being deliberately obtuse and loved nothing more than to rile Margarita up anytime he got the chance, something Margarita reciprocated.

"Your tux doesn't have to match, Diego," she told me directly. "If she wears purple like Fernando pointed out, the seamstress may make the corsage from violet, and you wear a purple tux or just a purple tie. I doubt you could pull that off. So, I suggest you ask her what color she's wearing."

"Do we have to match?" I asked. I didn't want to wear purple anything. It was my least favorite color, and I didn't think I would look good in it.

Margarita gave a long-suffering sigh. "No, Diego. You don't have to do anything. You don't have to rent the limo, buy the corsage, or anything like your cheapskate friend here suggested."

Fernando gave a V sign to show that he wasn't taking any of the words she had said to heart.

"So, I don't have to wear the purple tux?" I signed, trying to rile her up further. It worked; she looked ready to breathe fire.

"You know what? I'm done trying to help you. Plan your prom night yourself and see what your girlfriend says about it."

"So, limo, corsage, flowers, chocolate, and matching colors," I listed. "Anything else?"

"Having a chauffeur might be nice; it lends a sort of classiness to everything."

Fernando gave her a look that clearly said she was mistaken.

"Does he also need a valet as well as a footman? Or... footman and valet are the same, aren't they?" He looked to me for an answer, and I shrugged to say I had no idea.

If Margarita's glare could kill, Fernando would have been dead ten times over and in ten different ways.

"Valet?" I gestured at her, prompting her not to mind him and continue.

"That's all," Margarita replied.

Fernando gave a theatrical groan of relief. "Thank God for that. I was afraid he was going to have to go there with a magical fairy as well."

"I know you use flippancy to hide your nervousness because you're scared of girls. That's why you ditched prom and you're making fun of my suggestions. You want to be in Diego's shoes!"

"No, thanks. His shoes are too small for me. And I find most of the girls in Cutler High ditzy and frivolous."

Margarita stormed out, leaving us alone.

"Why do you antagonize her?" I demanded.

He gave me a sly grin. "It's fun. Margarita makes it easy." He cocked his head to the side, looking at me thoughtfully. "You aren't going to do what she suggested, are you?"

"Of course not, she was joking when she said that. There's no way she'd expect me to do all that without having money or a source of income."

"So, you're just going to leave it simple?"

"Sure. When you keep things simple, it's easier for them to never go wrong."

My tux didn't match Seema's dress as Margarita had advised, nor did I buy a bouquet or have a chauffeur. I also decided my Cavalier was good enough. I wore my black tux and purchased a single rose, a wrist corsage, and a small box of chocolates. They had all cost a reasonable amount, and since Seema wasn't like the other girls Margarita had mentioned, I thought she would be suitably impressed.

It was her brother Kamal who opened the door this time, with a scowl that drew deep, harsh lines into his face.

"You're Diego, right?" he demanded.

At my nod, he turned his head slightly to the side and hollered into the house, "Seema, your ride is here. Hurry up!"

There was a shout of something in return, and Kamal grinned.

"You might as well come in. It's going to take a while before she's ready. I don't know what she and Mom are up to, but they've been giggling for a while."

"Do you want some soda or chai?" he offered. I shook my head to signify no. Grunting, he went off to the kitchen and came back holding a bottle of beer. He collapsed on the couch and saluted me with the bottle.

I kept a small, polite smile on my face as I wondered if this was going to be a repeat of the last time I had been in Seema's house with her dad's passive-aggressive glare and threats. I glanced at Kamal; he seemed pleasant enough.

"You're deaf," he finally said, shocking me with his statement, leaving me bewildered as to how to react to his straightforwardness. "Seema said you couldn't—permanent hearing loss, yeah?"

I nodded.

"And you're unable to speak either. Must be tough," Kamal concluded at my nod, appearing sympathetic.

I shrugged. It wasn't that tough; I was born this way. It was my reality, and I had learned how to adapt to the world and circumstances around me.

"I wouldn't know what I would do if I were in your shoes. Dad would have probably abandoned me in the middle of nowhere. You have seen him, haven't you? Meanest man to ever walk this earth."

I wasn't sure how to respond. A part of me was glad I couldn't. I didn't think Kamal expected a response from me. One thing was sure, I had not liked my encounter with his father, and I didn't love my contact with Kamal. I wouldn't want to repeat them for anything.

"Are those for Seema?" he asked, lifting his chin to point at the box I was holding. At my nod, he went on. "Good choice. Seema loves gifts. Ah, there she is!"

Seema wore a pale blue dress of a wispy material; her hair pulled up from her face like you see women do in the movies for fancy occasions. She was wearing more makeup than she had on our first date and was breathless with anticipation. I thought I'd forgotten how to breathe. Her mom was beaming behind her.

"What a cute couple you are!" her mom exclaimed. She took a picture of us with Seema's phone.

"I'll send it to you," Seema promised before saying bye to her mom and brother.

"Have fun, little sis, and watch out for her, Diego," Kamal said to me, and I got the message. I nodded to tell him I would and opened the door for Seema to get in. I closed it after her, then hurried to the other side, got in, and drove off to school.

Prom was being held in the gym. As we approached, our arms linked, and I wished Fernando was with me. He would have found something funny to say to distract me from the sinking feeling in my gut. I didn't know what happened at proms. I wasn't interested in what happened. All I knew was that there would be music, dancing, and some voting for prom king and queen. If that was all prom was about, then it was highly overrated. I would choose a good game over it anytime. Seema didn't seem to share the same nervousness as I did. She was glowing with excitement.

It was warm in the gym, and my hearing aids picked and amplified the noise booming from the speaker, along with the din of murmurings. I knew then I wouldn't enjoy the night. Before it was over, I would be nursing a splitting headache. Even though I was skeptical about the night going great for me, I put on a smiling face for Seema's sake, although I could feel my mood gradually darkening, and the presence of Sebastian did nothing to make it better.

He looked like a monkey wearing a tight suit cutting off the circulation to his brain. It was mean and uncalled for, but I felt better as I imagined Sebastian doing tricks on my commands. He burst into derisive laughter when he saw us.

"Seema, you chose to come to senior prom with the dumb and deaf guy hanging from your arms? Wow, you surprise me."

Seema paid no attention to him, steering me in the direction of the punch bowl, which was manned by Mr. Hoffman to prevent students from tampering with it, I guessed. He brightened when he saw me, and his smile became knowing when he saw Seema was with me.

"Diego, Seema, how are you this fine evening?"

"Fine, Mr. Hoffman," she said, the tone of her voice indicating she was regretting bringing us to the punch bowl as I was regretting having come to the prom in the first place. It wouldn't be long before my head started to ache, and all I wanted was the comfort of home. Arranging the aisles in Fernando's uncle's store would have been more fun than this.

"Have fun you two," Mr. Hoffman said as Seema handed me a cup of punch and we turned to leave.

The punch was tart and too sweet. I felt nauseous after the first swallow. Seema tapped me to bring my attention to her and asked the question that made my palms sweaty.

"Wanna dance?"

I couldn't deny her. I could be a firecracker on the field, but I had two left feet on the dancefloor. After some awkward shuffling with the chaperones breathing down on our necks, we left the dancefloor. Seema had disappointment written all over her face. I resolved to try harder. She cheered up significantly when her friends came with their dates to join us. I was sent to get more punch and went gratefully, wishing for the night to be over. I would have loved it if we had gone on a date instead of this.

When I got back with more punch, her friends were still there, gushing about who had come with whom and playing fashion police. They drifted away, and I was left standing awkwardly with Seema—something that had never happened in our relationship before. I resented prom and whoever had thought up the ridiculous idea.

"Do you want to get out of here?" Seema asked me, and I perked up but pretended to think about it before I nodded. "Let's go," I signed.

We escaped to the soccer field for some time and sat down in the bleachers. Technically, we hadn't left the event. There were a couple of other couples there, hidden in the shadows. We sat in silence for some time. It wasn't a particularly comfortable silence, and I desperately wanted to tell her something, but she appeared distant, as if lost somewhere I couldn't reach her.

I was suddenly afraid I had ruined the night for her. I might have shown my displeasure in being here, and she had most likely noticed it. I knew I should try harder.

"It's a beautiful night," she finally said, breaking the remote silence, looking at me with a soft smile, and I felt like everything was all right.

"Are you cold?" I gestured. It was cooler outside than it had been in the gym.

Seema shook her head. "I feel fine. You aren't, are you? The noise was giving you a headache. I saw it in your eyes."

"It's nothing." I attempted to shrug it off, and Seema briefly accepted it.

"You're not enjoying the prom, is that right?" she inquired. That moment should have been when I should have said something along the lines of: *"It's cool, but I'd prefer if we were alone for the rest of the night,"* or anything than what I'd actually said.

The words that spelled my doom flowed from my fingers rapidly. "Yeah," I admitted. "I think prom is a stupid idea. Honestly, it would be more fun arranging cleaning products with Fernando."

I expected her to laugh at my words. Instead, she stiffened, and she immediately withdrew from me.

"I see," she said, her face cold and tense.

"Seema," I started to sign, but she slashed her hand through the air, stopping me from continuing and stood up.

"Well, I guess I shouldn't keep you two love birds alone anymore since it would be more fun to do stuff with Fernando than with me."

"I didn't mean…" I started gesturing again, but she had turned her back on me and was angrily striding for the gym.

I sprang up and went after her, admonishing myself for the poor way in which I had communicated myself. I had made it seem like her company was boring. For a person wearing heels, she moved fast and had already slipped in through the door before I got there. I entered, wincing at the new onslaught of loud sounds, but concentrated on finding Seema.

I saw her heading for the snack table and increased my pace, reaching out to touch her shoulder. She reacted violently, throwing my arm off, and what happened next was a blur. I guess I tripped and fell sideways against the punch bowl, which wobbled and splashed red liquid on her dress before smashing to the floor and splashing what remained of its content onto her. She slipped on the spilled punch and landed hard on her back.

Horrified, I moved to help her, but she screamed for me to leave her alone.

"Don't come near me, Diego!" Her face was hard and bitter. I stood there motionless, my face flaming from the amount of attention we were receiving. Sebastian appeared as if he had been summoned and dashingly helped her up. Embarrassment, guilt, and jealousy warred in me. I tried to go to her again, but Sebastian stopped me.

"She told you to stay away, Herrera! Have the decency to do what the lady asks! What are you all looking at if you aren't going to help?" he snarled at the crowd. At that point, he didn't look like Sebastian, the bully; he looked worried, concerned for her well-being, as if he was the good guy and I was somehow the bad one. Maybe I was since it had been because of me she had fallen.

Seema didn't look back at me, and I felt like gum scraped off the bottom of a shoe.

I waited until they disappeared, but I lurked back outside to the bleachers, taking the long route to the parking lot to get my car. I wanted to look for Seema and ask for a chance to explain myself, but I didn't. I drove off. I couldn't go home, not when Mom would be there waiting for me with an eager expression.

And then there would be Margarita with her slight mocking smile. Instead, I drove to the store where Fernando was working. He was at the counter when I entered.

"Hey, welcome to Cortez's, how can I help you?" he said with a saccharine smile.

"Very funny," I gestured, not amused.

"Hey!" He did a double take as if he had just noticed my appearance. "It's prom, dude, and you're here. Why are you here and not at prom with your girlfriend?"

I gave him a shortened version of what had happened.

"Dude," he said, and that word really said it all. I was glad he didn't say anything more than that; I didn't want him to tell me how stupid I was. "Do you want to buy tissues? I think you're about to start crying."

I made a rude gesture, and he laughed.

"Come on, I've been praying for a clean-up partner, and God has finally answered my prayers. But you might want to text Seema before you get lost in the back-breaking work."

His suggestion was sound, and I feverishly texted Seema. It was mostly incoherent babbling, but they all carried the same message: Are you all right? I'm sorry for ruining your night. Please forgive me.

Cleaning up wasn't that distracting, and I found myself checking my phone countless times for a response from her, even though I knew the phone would have vibrated if she had replied. I was going out of my mind wondering what was going on with her.

"Her brother would probably eat you alive if you showed up on their property," Fernando told me when I gestured that I wanted to check on her.

"I'll throw rocks at her window. I don't have to knock on

the front door," I insisted.

"Oh, for real? And how do you know where her room is? The rock hits the wrong window, and you'll be minced meat."

The rest of the weekend was agonizing. Seema never returned my texts, and I had sent a lot, each more desperate than the last.

Returning to school on Monday left me with mixed feelings. On the one hand, I would finally be able to apologize. On the other hand, half of the school had seen what had occurred, and I cringed every time I remembered that little scene. I couldn't believe that prom night had gone so wrong. If only I had thought twice before signing those words to Seema, she wouldn't have gotten upset and rushed back into the gym, the punch would have never crashed to the floor and splashed all over her, Seb wouldn't have taken her home, and I wouldn't be immersed in my negative thoughts.

"Chill, dude," Fernando said to me. I was squirming with anxiety. "The worst she could do is ignore you or slap you like she did when you guys first met. My money is on the slap."

She did neither. Instead, she chose to smile at me as if the prom incident had never happened.

I smiled back, feeling like the luckiest man in the world.

CHAPTER 9

I stared down at the message from Seema, feeling my heart sink.

"I'm sorry, but I won't be able to make it for our date. I have a headache. I am sincerely sorry, Diego. Forgive me?"

This time was the third date she had blown off, and I was starting to get the feeling she wasn't interested in our relationship anymore. The last time, she gave an excuse about having to watch the butcher shop on her dad's behalf. The time before that, she forgot she promised to help her mom with something. According to her, she was genuinely sorry. The time before that, she had cramps. Now, she had a headache. While I shouldn't jump to conclusions, the writing seemed to be on the wall.

Ever since the incident at prom, she had been reserved and distant. Although she was back to her usual self these past couple of days, I couldn't help but feel she wasn't all there. There was a massive elephant in the room that needed addressing, but we were both ignoring it.

Fernando had told me to talk to her, but she seemed so remote that any chance of broaching the subject of what had happened at prom would get me frozen out. So, I kept quiet and wished everything would go back to normal, something for which Fernando called me *tonto*. I knew I was stupid, but relationships were new to me, and I didn't want to worsen it more than I already had.

"So, you're happy to let it fester?" Fernando challenged, a look of disbelief on his face.

"It could also heal up if I leave it alone," I countered, signing.

"Que tonto," he stressed, shaking his head. "If you don't sort this out now, it's going to affect everything around you."

Fernando's prediction was right. These past couple of days, my concentration had been slacking in soccer practice, and Coach Miller had noticed. After warning me several times to get my head out of the clouds and back on the field where it belonged, he benched me until "I got my act together," a decision that shocked my teammates and me.

Fernando resisted saying I told you so and said at least I hadn't been kicked off the team. A small comfort. What was the point of being on a soccer team if I was only going to be watching from the sidelines? That the coach benched me was a substantial blow to my self-esteem, no doubt about that. But I was still immersed in the mystery of my girlfriend's aloofness. Not knowing whether she still liked me hurt, and I knew I would prefer breaking up than remaining in a state of uncertainty.

Sighing, I texted her back: *Sorry to hear that. Should I come over and kiss your headache better?*

Her reply was instant: *There's no need to, Diego. I took some ibuprofen. I'll sleep it off. I know, why don't you and Fernando go on a guy date so the ticket doesn't go to waste?*

I couldn't help but smile at her choice of words. Fernando would freak out if he saw the text referring to our hangouts as a date. *I will do that. Are you sure you are okay?*

Yeah, don't worry about me. I'll be fine, and I'll have company. Seb is coming over so we can work on the chemistry project together.

My heart clenched as I studied her message. Seb. Sebastian Cliffe, my enemy, was going to be at my girlfriend's house. I shouldn't be torturing myself this way since it was only for a science project, but the thought of Sebastian together with Seema working on a chemistry project wasn't a pleasant image. I couldn't help but notice she and Sebastian had grown closer since prom night. Sebastian had taken her home that night, showing a gentleman side to him that I never thought existed. Who knows what they had discussed as he drove her to her house. But the following Monday, they were walking together, looking like close friends. Fernando had given me a sad, pitying look as if he knew something I didn't yet. That look had irritated me.

In a way, I was angry with Seema. My life had been peaceful and blissfully mundane until she slapped me, and her waltzing herself into my existence had brought about turmoil. But she wasn't solely to blame. If I had acted like Fernando, the flash I'd felt when she had first smiled at me would have fizzled out to nothing. Instead, I had let the spark turn into a flame and fanned it into the burning inferno that was now consuming me.

Mom and Margarita had noticed there was something wrong. Still, I didn't say anything, offering as an excuse that the coach was working us to the bone in practice, but Margarita guessed too close to the truth for my comfort. The last thing I needed was her jeering commentary. She had been in a light mood for a week now. I guess her dealer was out of jail and back to supplying her regularly with her fix.

"Trouble in paradise," she quipped with her little jeering smile, but the strength of my glare burnt it from her lips, and she raised her hands in surrender. "Just joking, Diego." Through the rest of the dinner, she kept throwing me wary glances.

I had never exhibited any sign of anger all the time she had known me, and here I was glaring at her. I didn't know what she had seen in my eyes, but I guessed it had been enough to keep her on her toes around me for a few days until she reverted to her usual jeering self.

I didn't tell Mom the coach benched me for the rest of the season or that I got a C in Mr. Hoffman's pop quiz, the first inconsistency in my grade since elementary. I was as surprised as he had been when he handed me back my quiz, highlighting the part where my mistake lay. Mr. Hoffman later called me into his office and asked if there was anything wrong. He had caught me spacing out in class, which was highly irregular as I was usually always attentive. Mr. Rodriguez, the history teacher, also told him I had done a messy job in the assignment he had given.

"Are there problems at home?" he asked. "Are you in some kind of trouble? Do you need to speak with the guidance counselor?"

I had shaken my head and told him I had been feeling a bit sick for a while now, but I was better, and everything would change. It hadn't seemed like he believed me, but he thankfully didn't press, and I left his office feeling worse. First soccer, now my grades were slipping.

"You have to break it off with her," Fernando told me while I tried and failed to beat him at chess. His little diablo was purring contentedly on his lap.

"Or at least talk to her if you are interested in keeping the relationship. But I recommend breaking it off, like chopping off a gangrenous arm before it infects the entire body."

I didn't appreciate him referring to Seema or our relationship as gangrene, but I knew he was right. But I wasn't keen on breaking if off, still clinging to the hope that everything would somehow be all right.

I texted Fernando and asked if he would like to meet up at the bowling alley.

Sure, came his instant reply. *Just give me an hour. I'm trying to bathe Gordo.*

I winced in sympathy, knowing how much Gordo hated baths as much as he hated me. He didn't want us to dunk him in water, so he fended us off with everything he had. I had once had the misfortune of assisting Fernando in bathing him, and that ranked second in the top ten worst days of my life.

Good luck, I texted him and went into the house to shower. I had just returned from practice, and there was still no improvement in my performance. The coach had said nothing, but his expression had said it all: he was thoroughly disappointed in me. So, a dark cloud hovered over me as I ate an apple and drove to Capitol Bowl in West Sacramento.

Fernando was already there, and he was bearing apparent marks of Gordo's struggle.

"What happened?" Fernando asked as we changed footwear. "I thought you and Seema were supposed to go on a date—a rejuvenation date as you put it. She blew you off again, huh?"

I didn't have to respond.

"Come on, Diego," he said, changing the subject. "Let me show you why they call me the bowling king."

I cracked a smile as I signed back. "Nobody calls you that."

"They might start from today on," he replied cockily.

We were at the bowling alley for a while, and Fernando showed me why they called him the bowling jester. His mishaps amused me, and I was sure he was struggling on purpose to take my mind off Seema. It worked like a charm; the dark mood I had been in dissipated.

We took a break an hour later to buy bottles of water at the vending machine. After it ate Fernando's dollar without dispensing the water, I fed it my dollar, and grumbling about luck, he retrieved both bottles.

"Should we go to the movies? Henry was saying something about a horror movie."

Since I had no other plans, I told him yes, and we drove to the movies. I was about to turn off the engine when Fernando asked me to keep it running.

"We might need to leave here quickly."

"Why? You want to vandalize the building?" I raised an amused brow at him but stopped at the serious look on his face. With a nod of his head, he gestured out his window. I looked and wished I could have unseen what I saw. The ibuprofen had worked like magic. Or maybe it had been dear Seb's presence or the fact Seema seemed to have recovered from her debilitating headache. She was laughing and beaming at Sebastian, who had an arm around her waist in a way that denoted they were something more than just friends. My happy mood dimmed, then went out with a wink. My hands were trembling, and it was becoming harder to breathe. Yet I couldn't tear my eyes away from the scene before me.

Inhaling deeply and exhaling a shaky breath, I gathered the tattered robe of my composure and cocked my head in a questioning way at Fernando. *Shall we leave?* my expression asked.

"Sure. My place. Gordo is on a prowl for lady cats, so you don't have to worry about him yowling and hissing at you."

I drove us back, resisting the urge to pound at the steering wheel until my hands were bloody or drive the car into the nearest pole. Fernando snuck glances at me from the corner of his eye, but he was mercifully quiet. With a straight, unbothered face,

I kept my eyes on the road.

There was no one at his place when we got there, and it smelled strongly of the vanilla-scented soap Fernando had used to bathe his cat. I took my seat on his bed and looked straight at him.

"You knew they'd be there," I gestured.

Fernando had moved his chair from his study desk and straddled it, facing me.

"I heard Sebastian tell one of his friends they'd be going on a date to the movies yesterday. And I knew that in order for her to be there, she'd have to cancel on you, so I planned to take you there."

"Why didn't you tell me when you heard?"

"I thought you'd stop speaking to me if I said such 'malicious' lies about your girlfriend," he told me.

"What makes you think I won't stop speaking to you now?" It was just a question. I would never stop speaking to my best friend over something so trivial. I felt oddly drained of all emotion. I was just tired.

Fernando shrugged. "Just make sure you give me back that book I loaned to you when you do."

I couldn't even spare a smile at his quip.

"I guess this is the end," I gestured, then sighed before taking out my phone from the pocket of my hoodie. I had to make some changes. The picture Seema's mom had taken of us was my wallpaper, reminding me of a time before everything fell apart. First things first, I would have to change it and delete the picture.

I thought for a moment how to end it and then decided to be straightforward. *It's over,* I texted. *You'll be happier with Seb.* And send.

"Are you all right?" Fernando asked me.

I nodded, and then I shook my head in the negative.

"But I'll be okay," I promised, gesturing at him. "Who's ever died from heartache?" It was meant to be flippant, but it didn't strike the right chord, as Fernando gave a half-hearted smile.

"Do you want to do anything? Whoop you at chess? We could go hunting for Gordo. You name it, anything you want," he offered. I wished he would stop talking.

Shaking my head, I switched off my phone, slipped it into my pocket, and then kicked off my high-tops before lying on the bed.

"I guess I'll just go to sleep, and when I'm awake—"

"It's not going to go away like a bad dream, Diego," Fernando said. I felt a flash of irritation at him. I wasn't trying to pretend it was.

"When I'm awake," I repeated, as though he hadn't interrupted me, "we can play chess before your uncle returns. It's poker night."

Fernando's grin was the last thing I saw before I closed my eyes. I felt a sense of relief it was all over. At that moment, I wished I could go back to the way my life was before she had waltzed in.

CHAPTER 10

Between us, on the table, there was a scattered pile of documents and two cups of iced tea. Antonio's was one of our all-time favorite places to go. They made the best pizzas in town. Fernando sat opposite me, his elbows resting on the tiny corner of the desk not covered by papers, propping up his face, a pencil clenched between his teeth. He looked as if he was thinking painful thoughts and went on thinking for two more minutes before making a frustrated and defeated noise. Fernando took the pencil into his hand and canceled out a word that he had previously written with great vengeance. Then he tossed the pencil away, slumped in his seat, and folded his arms across his chest.

"I just can't make a choice," he said with an air of despair.

"But I thought you had decided on Brown University," I gestured.

He gave the paper before him a look full of loathing. Then he looked up to say, "I had thought so as well, but after thinking about it carefully, Mom would nail my feet to the ground before letting me go that far."

"San Bernardino Valley College?"

He transferred the look of disgust to me. "Too close to home."

"But it's not Sacramento," I pointed out, but he ignored me.

"You had thirty colleges on the shortlist, Fernando. Are you saying none of them is the 'perfect' college for you?"

"That's exactly what I'm saying."

I rolled my eyes at him. We had been on this all afternoon. He had texted me after I finished soccer practice that he needed my help for some emergency and asked if I would please meet him at Antonio's. I had changed into my clothes and rushed over to find him stressing over lists.

"I'd have to consider the tuition," he went on. "How far away it is from home, etcetera, and etcetera. I don't want to spend the golden years of my adult life working off student loans. I'm not like you, my lucky friend. Between your big brains and your shining soccer career, you could land a full scholarship that will take care of everything for you."

"What golden years?" I signed.

"True, true," he mused before returning to his paper.

I picked up my drink and leaned back, when movement caught my eye; I looked up just in time to see Seema and her friend, Sandra, enter. Our eyes met and held before I looked away and focused on the view outside. There was nothing to see except for cars and people walking. It wasn't fascinating, but I continued watching.

It had been two weeks since I had broken up with Seema, and my life had gone back to the way it had been before I had met her. My grades had picked up again, causing Mr. Hoffman to stop giving me pitying looks, and I was back to myself on the field. But even after two weeks of exceptional performance, Coach Miller still didn't relent in his punishment.

I think he wanted the message to sink in, and I deserved it, so I bore it quietly. I tried not to think about Seema in those two weeks. That we were in almost the same classes didn't help matters, especially because she seemed to want to talk to me. I hadn't given her the chance, and for the first time in my life, I was glad I was deaf so I didn't have to hear her calling out to me as I strode away. Fernando had been supportive during the fourteen days of heartache, devising new ways to distract me.

As much as I tried not to think about her, it wasn't easy. She was my first love. Mom told me those things don't go away easily, and there were often lingering feelings even if a decade had passed. I wanted it to go away so badly. I was glad high school would be over soon. I couldn't wait to go to college and begin a new chapter of my life, although there were things I would miss from my high school life. Fernando, for one.

We wouldn't be going to the same college seeing as he wanted to put as much distance between himself and downtown Sacramento as physically possible. He was exploring all viable options. I wanted to be closer to home and already had a college in mind. I knew Mom would feel more comfortable if I was only a few hours away. With so many problems at home, being thousands of kilometers away seemed careless and irresponsible. What if she and Miguel needed me?

I would miss the soccer team. I had grown close to my teammates, and I could call them friends. The team had nurtured my talents and honed them, turning me into a better player.

Finally, deciding I'd had enough of the same scene, I looked away to find Fernando staring at me.

"She came in just now, didn't she?" he asked, and I nodded. Before I could stop him, he craned his neck about in search of her. "I think she left. Coward."

Fernando was right. She probably had left the moment I looked away. I felt an indescribable feeling.

"What do you think of Centura College? It's in Virginia,"

Fernando said, carrying on with our conversation as if there had been no pause or interruptions.

"Is it far away enough for you?" I asked.

"Well, it's not the moon. I'll make a new list and put this one on top." He worked steadily for five minutes before looking up and asking, "Have you decided your major?"

"What are you, a cop?" I gestured.

"I'll pass that righteous mantle to others who deserve it. So, still going to be a healer of the body?"

"Well, I don't know yet. Maybe Literature since I like books."

"Why not microbiology?"

"I'm not interested in being in school forever," I gestured.

Fernando laughed. It felt like more of a snigger, though.

"I haven't decided yet," I confessed, making a face as I signed.

"Well, you have a lot of time to decide."

I picked up a blank paper and started folding it into an origami crane.

"The semi-final is going to be next Saturday, right?"

I nodded yes.

"And Coach Miller still has you benched?"

I paused my origami-making to reply to him. I told him it was Coach Miller's way of keeping me on my toes and that he would unbench me soon.

I thought Fernando looked skeptical, but couldn't be sure.

"Why not take a gap year?" I asked him when I finished with my origami. It looked misshapen.

"And you'll fund it?" Fernando retorted.

"You could sell your camera. Together with your savings, you should be able to come up with a couple hundred."

"Which would see me as far as New York and leave me there. Stop talking nonsense Diego and help me with this list."

"What do you think I've been doing?"

"I don't know. Making an odd-looking paper turtle?"

I threw the crane at him.

I remained on the bench up until game night, to my great shock and resentment. Coach Miller continued being adamant with his punishment, even after Sean pointed out I was needed since Zach was still reeling from food poisoning. Surely, he wouldn't risk them losing to teach me a lesson.

As incredulous as it might be, it seemed that was Coach Miller's goal. He wanted the team to fail so I could see the consequences of not keeping my head in the game. Soccer was a world of its own, untouched by the drama from the outside. You were either in or out—no middle ground. I understood his aim and realized it would eventually come to bite him in the butt.

We had been on a winning streak, and the entire team was reborn. If we lost this game because Coach Miller refused to let a talented player play, he might have a revolt on his hands. For most of us, it was our last semester in high school, and we wanted to win a trophy before we left. It was our goal, and the fact that Coach Miller would let our hard work and dream go down the drain was unacceptable.

Sean had argued with him after the last practice before the game. Their voices grew steadily louder and louder until Coach Miller had blown the whistle. The sharp, penetrating noise amplified by my hearing aids made my head hurt.

"Herrera will remain on the bench for the rest of the season. Anyone who has a problem with my decision is free to quit the team now."

Coach Miller was unreasonable. But even if they had wanted to quit in the heat of the moment, it was too late.

My stomach was in a knot on the first night of the game. It wasn't about my performance; it was about the entire team's. We were going to lose the game because of my foolishness and Coach Miller's obstinateness. Great! What a way to end high school, with the guilt that I had denied the team a chance to hoist a trophy.

My teammates put up a brave fight the first half of the game, but with Zach feeling out of sorts, there was a dissonance in their almost-perfect rhythm, a crack our opponents readily exploited. It was agonizing watching from the bench, knowing I could have prevented that, done that differently, which had been what Coach Miller wanted.

"All right, Hudson?" Coach Miller demanded from Zach after the referee had blown the whistle signifying the end of the first half.

Pale and covered in sweat, Zach nodded. "Sure thing, Coach."

The second half was even worse to watch, but thanks to the defense and the goalkeeper, the opponent still had only a goal under their belt. But our back was slowly weakening. It was only a matter of time before they won another, or the time elapsed.

About ten minutes into the game, Zach suddenly collapsed, and I shot up from my seat in worry and anticipation. This was my opportunity. The coach couldn't deny me the chance to re-join my teammates. The medics carried Zach off the field on a stretcher, and the team was returning to us.

Coach Miller turned, and I was trembling with anticipation as I thought I would see his lips form the words: *Herrera, you're up. Don't disappoint me out there, kid.* But instead, he looked past me to Mitch.

Mitch was an almost permanently benched player. He was passionate about soccer but lacked the innate talent for it. Even though he trained as hard as everyone else did, he was still the weakest player. At that point, I was afraid Coach Miller was going to pick him to show me that hard work sometimes trumped raw talent.

"You can't be serious, Coach!" Sean exploded, his sweaty face hard with anger. "They're tearing us to pieces out there, and we have an injured player on our hands, and you want Mitch to fill in! No offense, Mitch."

Mitch shrugged to show the words hadn't stung.

"Come on, Coach! You want to win as badly as we do, and we can't win without Herrera! Believe me, he's learned his lesson. And if he hasn't, I'll resign as captain and quit the team altogether!"

I gaped at Sean, shocked he would stake that much on me. He wasn't looking at me. Instead, he was glaring fiercely at Coach Miller whose thoughts were written plainly on his face. There was a brief war between him keeping me on the bench and him letting me play. The blast of the whistle made his mind up for him.

"Fine, Herrera. Give it your best out there. Don't fail me."

My grin could have lit up the world.

I did give my best out there on the field, surrounded by my teammates whom I trusted. They seemed to have gained some energy from my presence, and we moved together as a team. There were no distractions. Every spectator was mute. They were ready to burst like a dam and wash over us when it was all over.

After half an hour, I found myself being tackled to the

ground by jubilant team members as they piled themselves on me. Through the spaces, I could see Coach Miller pumping his fist in the air, beyond psyched. Before it became too uncomfortable, they lifted themselves off me and pulled me up for a celebratory jig.

But this wasn't the end; there was still the last game. We weren't worried. We would crush it, just as we had all others. It felt like the world was ours for the taking.

CHAPTER 11

Mom wore a new dress for my graduation. It had been years since she had bought anything for herself. I was happy for her. The dress was straightforward and inexpensive. She had bought it at Gap and spent half an hour ironing it. Through the ceremony, she had a handkerchief pressed to her face to stifle sobs.

Dad had come along with her, Margarita and Miguel, despite saying he might not make it, leading to an argument between him and Mom. We closed the door to our room to drown out the noise and played cards until Mom called us for dinner. He was also wearing his best suit, and the expression on his face was one of torture. There was nothing in the world that Dad disliked more than long ceremonies. As a result, he stayed away from weddings. He even skipped Margarita's graduation. Mom was determined he wouldn't skip mine, however. Seated behind them was Fernando's family, also wearing their best. My eyes went over them and came back to Margarita.

She had also graduated from Cutler High. I wondered how she must have felt returning here. Mom had wept on her graduation day, too, soaking her new dress in tears. Margarita had changed a lot since the day she had graduated. She had left high school, a bright-eyed girl, ready to make her mark on the world and returned as someone broken and sad.

As our class president gave her speech on the Plexiglas podium, I let my eyes rove the gym, drinking in the sights one last time. The faces of the teachers, our stern but proud principals, the students in my graduating class, and their parents. I spotted Coach Miller, wearing a suit instead of his sweat clothes with his baseball cap. He met my gaze before giving me a nod, and I smiled at him.

The final game had been last week. The emotions I had felt that day still lingered. Together with the sweet sorrowful feeling of leaving a place I had spent so many years, it created a cocktail of intense, almost positive emotions. We had won the game and the trophy.

"Party at my place!" Sean had yelled out of the blue. We had piled ourselves into various cars, making a ruckus as we went.

The music at the party was so loud it gave me a splitting headache, but I didn't care, pumped as I was from the adrenaline of the game. I downed glass after glass of tequila until I passed out on the couch and woke up feeling sick several times. I woke with a headache, hunger pangs, and nausea, but I wouldn't have spent that night any other way.

We all applauded when the class president was through with her speech, and then the principal gave his speech too. His was shorter, telling us how proud he was of us and that he and the teachers had done their best to prepare us for the world out there. He gave us advice on how to tackle problems and embrace change before concluding with wishing us good luck and all the best.

Fernando gestured to me that if he had honestly wished us well, he would have given every one of us a check. I smiled at his joke.

When my name was called to receive my high school diploma, I thought I heard Mom yell, and when I turned, she was smiling and crying all at the same time. Fernando's uncle had his digital camcorder hoisted up to record the event. I smiled at them all.

Principal Harris shook my hand, smiling at me as he handed me the diploma. He announced that I was one of the best students Cutler High had seen, graduating early at sixteen with a perfect 4.0 GPA after skipping a total of two grades—once in elementary school and once at Cutler High. "Without a doubt, Diego Herrera is a brilliant young man," he said, adding he was proud to have been able to cultivate the mind of a bright young man like me and wished me good luck in all my endeavors. Mom sobbed harder into her handkerchief. She was beyond proud of me. I was proud of myself too.

⸙

Fernando had finally decided on the college he was going to attend. With a very smug smile, he told me he'd chosen the University of Philadelphia. He had announced this when we were on his porch a day after our graduation ceremony. As I stared at him, I felt a pang. In a short while, we wouldn't be sitting next to each other, chatting easily. The selection committee had decided which institution I would attend. It wasn't what I'd had in mind before, but it was an offer I couldn't pass up.

I had won a full-tuition soccer scholarship to the University of Oregon in Eugene, Oregon. I had been glad for the offer, as it would ease the burden of tuition off my parents' already occupied shoulders. I jumped at it without a second thought. Everything seemed settled.

"We'll still see each other," Fernando said reassuringly after I told him what I'd been thinking. "We're just going off to college, not off the face of the earth. We'll text, write emails, probably drive miles to visit. There's Christmas, Easter, and Thanksgiving," he listed. "Loads of opportunities to see each other."

"But it won't be like before."

"Yeah, there's that part, but it's part of the change, part of growing up and moving on. We can either embrace the change or reject it," Fernando said, quoting from Principal Harris' speech.

My phone vibrated in my pocket, and I pulled it out. It was a text from Sean inviting us for a final soccer game at school. He asked me to bring Fernando along.

"Sure," Fernando readily agreed when I told him. "We aren't doing anything here. Let's go."

Sean had invited a bunch of other people as well, none of which were Sebastian, thank God, and with Fernando and me, we made twenty-two. We conducted draws to pick teams after Sean started hoarding the good players. I ended on the opposite side of Sean. After the players decided, I was promptly elected captain of the blue team. There was no time for a pep talk before the referee blew the whistle.

Since it was just a fun game and half of the players only played soccer as a hobby, we allowed some mild, cheap tricks to win. And after one of Sean's players used psychological warfare to win, my team employed it as well. We played until we were tired, which was a long time. There was no clear winner, as we kept arguing on which was a foul or not. Overall, it was an enjoyable experience, and I was glad Sean had thought of it, even though I ached all over.

I was grinning as I hobbled my way over to the bleachers where Fernando was seated. He had taken a shot to the head sometime earlier, and as a result, had to quit the game.

"Are you okay?" I asked him with my fingers.

"Sure, my vision has stopped blurring and doubling every-thing, though my temple still feels tender." He probed at it and winced.

"You need an ice pack for that. Come on, let's say bye to Sean and then go." I was sweaty and dirty from the field and sorely needed a shower and food—or food and a shower.

"There's going to be a party when we're done here," Sean said when Fernando and I went to tell him goodbye.

"Trust me... this was more celebration than I can take," Fernando said.

"Wimp," Sean accused with a smile. "See you around then, Cortez, Herrera."

"That's a sure thing, Hartford," Fernando said with a smile.

I gave a wave. Smiling broadly, I tried to convey all the grati-tude I felt into my smile before turning away, leaving the rowdy crowd behind. Fernando and I walked to the parking lot in com-panionable silence. Mom had promised chicken for dinner, and I was having pleasant thoughts about that until I saw Seema lean-ing against my car.

All at once, I felt angry and helpless, and when I turned to Fernando, he gave me a shrug and an expression that read: *don't look at me; that's your burden to bear.* Exhaling slowly, I resumed my walk, Fernando trailing behind me so I wouldn't see the grin on his face. I was glad I couldn't. I would probably have taken a swing at him if I did. Seema's frown transformed into an uncer-tain smile as she saw me, and she stood upright, a hopeful ex-pression in her hazel eyes. I won't deny the pang I felt, but I also wouldn't make the same mistake twice.

"Hi," she said softly, her words accompanied by a small wave.

For a moment, I struggled between being curt and being polite. I settled for just plain tired like I felt.

"What do you want, Seema?" I gestured. Fernando was staying out of this, so it was just between us.

"We need to talk," she said, her eyes shifting to Fernando, who was keeping himself behind me.

"No, we don't. Now would you please move away from my car? I need to use it."

She ignored my latter statement. The tip of her tongue darted out to swipe at her bottom lip. Once upon a time, that would have evoked a reaction from me. Maybe it did again, but I was just exhausted.

"Yes, we do!" she insisted. "You broke up with me without an explanation. I feel like I deserve an explanation, Diego, and I deserve the chance to explain myself also."

I was beginning to feel irritated. What could Seema possibly want to explain?

"There's no need, Seema. We've been broken up for weeks, and you're with Sebastian, that's explanation enough. Now would you please leave?" I gestured.

"Sebastian and I broke up."

"I'm sorry that happened to you."

She glanced sharply from my fingers to my face to see if I meant that or was being flippant.

"I didn't mean to hurt you, Diego. I love you. I don't know what happened."

No amount of signing could convey the loathing I felt for her, the load of hurt I felt, and the hovering cloud of feelings I had for her. I kept silent.

"Diego, I'm sincerely sorry. I shouldn't have done what I did that night at prom and with Sebastian. It was wrong of me, and I apologize. If there is anything I can do to make you forgive me, I will. I'd like us to put this behind us and try to be friends or even acquaintances if you want."

I smiled; I had to. Seema's apology now had the same note as the apology she had given me after she had slapped me. Then, I had been eager. Now, I was just tired.

"There is something you can do for me, Seema," I began to sign, and her eager hopeful expression amused me. "You can move away from my car," I finished saying and heard a sound from behind me.

Fernando must have laughed as Seema's eyes flashed behind me, bright with rage.

"If it hadn't been for *you*," she hissed at Fernando. "You turned him against me!" she accused. "Diego, please, I—"

We would never know the end of that conversation. I glared at her, the same glare that had stopped Margarita from continuing with her jeer. It also prevented Seema from completing her statement. I jerked my head irritably to the side, and Seema stepped away from my car, keeping a wary eye on me.

"I never thought you could be so cold, Diego." She delivered her final statement, but I was paying no attention to her, having already written her off in my head.

"Shall we?" I turned to Fernando, gesturing the words.

"Sure, dude."

She was still standing in the parking lot as I drove, and I tried not to watch her in the rear-view mirror as the car moved farther and farther from her. Fernando had no such qualms.

"She doesn't know where you live, does she? She seems in the mood to come after you and give you another slap on the face. Bye-bye, Diego."

I lifted my hands from the steering to sign, "Us, Fernando.

She hates your guts."

"Dude! Look where you're going and put your hands back on the steering wheel. Are you trying to kill us?"

I smiled at his agitation but obliged him. I drove him to his place first, and after telling him I would be over later in the evening, I drove back to my home and killed the engine. The image of chicken had reasserted itself into my mind, and I salivated in anticipation.

I was climbing up to the porch when the door burst open violently, and Margarita came out, scowling fiercely and carrying her duffle bag. Her eyes were red from weeping, tear tracks on her glowering face.

Her sudden and violent appearance had startled me. I quickly recovered and went after her as she went down the short flight of steps and came close enough to tap her shoulder. She whirled about, her duffel bag connecting with my chest. It hurt, and I grunted as I was forced to give a few inches.

"What's wrong? Where are you going?" I demanded.

Margarita started saying something, then shook her head and vociferated, "I just need to be away, Diego, from her." She had said "her" with such venom, it stunned me.

What had happened between her and Mom in the few hours I'd been gone? Since the night she had disappeared for three days, Mom had taken care not to incite another argument. Margarita had also taken enough care not to push Mom too hard. There had been months of peace. What could have happened to make her want to leave? Had those months just been the calm before the storm?

"Why? What happened?"

"Nothing you would understand, mama's boy."

I flinched at her words. She was hurt and in yet another one of her emotional rages, but I wished she wouldn't lash out at me, using me as her punching bag. I could feel a headache coming up, and I was exhausted and irritated with her behavior.

"Where are you going?" I signed with a calmness I wasn't feeling.

"To people who appreciate me!"

My temper was rising as well. "You mean people like Raquel, who keep you in a constant supply of drugs and aren't looking out for you like we are?"

She seemed taken aback by my retort as if she had never imagined I would talk to her like that. She recovered, and her lips spread in a jeering smile.

"Well, well. Dieguito finally grew up."

"You're acting like a spoiled brat," I signed.

She looked at my fingers like they were some poisonous snake, stiffened at the words I had signed before nodding and turning to leave. I didn't bother calling after her. I just watched her walk away with a calm I didn't feel before going inside.

Mom was pretending to read a magazine when I entered.

"Diego, you're back!" she said in a high voice.

"Yes, Mom," I signed back at her, and then shuffled towards my room to drop my bag.

Miguel was there, huddled on my bed. "Is she gone? Margarita? Is she gone?"

I nodded to answer his question.

"Margarita and Mom were arguing really bad. I tried to stop it, but they didn't pay attention to me. Dad just came in, saw them fighting, and walked out. He didn't try to do anything," Miguel reported.

That part of his narrative seemed to have genuinely shocked him more out of all that had happened.

"Mom tried to hit Margarita, but she held her hand. For a second, I thought she was going to hit Mom back, but she didn't. She only came in here to grab her duffle bag, and then she called someone named Joe."

He wrinkled his nose at the name as if it was distasteful. "She's not coming back, is she?"

I shrugged. I didn't know whether she would. She and Mom had had their arguments in the past, and she had stormed out only to return a few days later. This time might be the same, or it might be different.

"I don't want her to come back. She makes Mom cry a lot."

I had no answer for him and instead moved to the bathroom to have my shower. The cold water eased my headache a bit. When I was done, I put on new clothes and went to see Mom, having decided I had delayed it enough. She was still sitting in the same place and had not turned a single page of the magazine she had been pretending to read. The only difference was the tear stains that dotted the page.

"Oh Diego," she said as I sat by her. She leaned her head on my shoulder, crying.

The incident had shredded the dream of eating chicken. There was no way Mom was in the frame of mind to cook, and I couldn't leave her, so I ordered pizza. As I waited for it to arrive, I sat with her, holding her hand.

CHAPTER 12

I stared from the glossy magazines about conspiracy theories in Fernando's hands and up to his face, then glared at his mischievous smile before mouthing, "No." He knew how much I disliked them.

"Why not?" He had the audacity to look offended. "It's a thoughtful goodbye gift. You like reading, don't you?"

"Not this," I signed indignantly. "Tear the magazines up and toss them into the recycling bin. Better yet, burn them. I'll help."

"Hey!" Fernando protested. "My uncle gave them to me, but I, in my infinite wisdom, did think you might need them."

"For what exactly, kindling?" I demanded from him, signing.

He looked down at the glossy cover before replying. "Maybe. They'll burn nicely."

I threw my left shoe at him, and he disappeared beneath a pile of books. Gordo meowed his displeasure at being startled, then fixed his insolent stare on me before hopping off the bed and onto the window sill before proceeding to give himself a tongue bath.

We were in Fernando's room all afternoon, sorting through his worldly possessions, separating those he wanted to take along with him to college and those he would be leaving behind or giving away. So far, we had three piles: one for things Fernando was taking with him, another for things he was leaving behind, and the third for things he wasn't sure whether he wanted to leave behind or take with him.

"Are you sure you want to take this with you?" I gestured when he surfaced, a trace of laughter still on his face. I dangled his old camera in front of him.

He snatched it from my hand, looking down at it with a wistful expression before shaking his tiny fist in my face. "I can't give it away. Sentimental value. That was the first camera I ever owned. Need I remind you I bought it myself with the money I saved up from Christmas and mowing mean people's unkempt lawns?"

"Leave it behind then," I signed.

"For Mom to toss out? I swear, that woman is going to come in here when I'm gone with a vacuum cleaner and give everything I leave behind to the Salvation Army."

I wondered if Mom was going to do the same when I was gone. I didn't think she would. I could picture her sitting on my bed and going through the rest of my things with a sad smile. That image seemed more like my mom than her wielding a vacuum cleaner.

I remembered how frantic she had been when I had gone to the campus for a three-day orientation. I had almost thought she wouldn't let me leave with the way she had been asking if it had been vital for me to go. I understood why she had been so protective of me. She was wondering what was going to happen to me the moment I was far away from her, how the world was going to react to me when I was away from the little safety box she had built for me in downtown Sacramento.

I had no answer to soothe her fray nerves, but I knew I couldn't be her little Diego forever. I had to see what the world had in store for me. With Margarita gone now, it had made her even more determined to keep me close. If she could, she would probably stop me from going to college.

It had taken Dad's intervention to make her stop fretting. He had made plans with his friend, Lupe, to drive me to Eugene, Oregon, but the man couldn't bring me back. I had told him it was okay; I would make my way back home. Dad seemed to trust that I could take care of myself, but Mom didn't.

She and Dad had a brief and silent argument about his decision to let me go. I had seen his lips move to form the word *"silencio"* and thought I hadn't heard him say it in a while. That had ended the argument, and he had turned to inform me that Lupe would be ready for me in the morning, and I wouldn't need to make my way back myself. He had bought a bus ticket with which I was to return.

I would have liked Guillermo, Fernando's uncle, to have driven me to Oregon, but he had taken Fernando to his orientation in Philadelphia. So, I was stuck with corpulent Lupe, who had a Cheetos addiction and listened to loud norteño music that made my head hurt.

The drive to Oregon was roughly 475 miles, the trip taking seven hours. I had never been more than a thirty-minute drive away from home before. I felt both apprehensive at this change to my life and equally excited. I felt alive. We had left the day before orientation was to start and got to Eugene sometime around past four—seven hours too many in Lupe's company.

I could never understand how he and Dad had become friends. Their personalities were as different as the sun and moon. I had never been so furious with a person my entire life. He had treated me like I was a brainless child because of my disabilities. Most of the time, I had just looked away from him, nursing the headache caused by the music.

When we stopped at the gas stations to fill his Volvo up, I wandered away to the toilet and pondered on the merit of hitch-hiking my way to Eugene. I had my ticket back and a couple of dollars to eat and could probably rent a room in a motel. But remembering how worried Mom would be if Lupe had returned to report me missing, I banished the devilish thoughts and returned to Lupe.

He had previously booked a room in a motel for me to spend the three nights if I wasn't going to stay in the dorm. We shared the same room for our first and last night together in Eugene, but thankfully, it had come with two single beds. Exhausted from the journey, I had gone to bed without eating and woken up at six the following morning, trembling with nervous energy. Lupe had woken two hours later, and after getting ready at his own slow pace, he had driven me to the campus and left. For the first time in my life, I had been alone—no Mom, no Dad, and no Fernando—tossed into the wild.

It had been the scariest and most exciting three days of my life. I felt freedom, and I was too nervous and curious about everything to be lonely. Fernando had told me he had felt the same way when I had returned. He had already made two friends and signed up for the Red Cross and the Journalist Club. He had also met his roommate. I had gone to check the hall the university had assigned to me, as well as my room, but I hadn't met my roommate. It was the same size as the room I shared with Miguel and Margarita, though much nicer. I didn't spent my night there, choosing instead to return to the motel and spend hours writing in the journal I had bought.

I signed up for the Mexican Students' Association (MSA) and went to check out the soccer field. I couldn't wait to play on it. I daydreamed of all the soccer games and matches I was going to play there and could hear the cheering of the crowd as I made the winning goal.

"It's a cool school," I signed after concluding with my tale.

"Ditto," Fernando said.

"You can give the camera to Miguel. I think he's been bitten by the photography bug as well," I suggested.

Fernando looked thoughtful at my suggestion. "Well, he can have it, but I'm not sure it's still working."

Miguel was also interested in breaking things apart to see how they worked. I wasn't going to tell Fernando that; he would probably have an aneurysm. I was going to give Miguel the wooden flute that had belonged to Abuelo Carlos before he had passed. Mom had given it to me as a gift for my tenth birthday for reasons I did not know. It wasn't as if I could play it. It had been gathering dust in my drawer for years, and since Miguel would be far better at music than I was, he would make better use of it than I did.

"Does Miguel like leather pants? I don't know what I was thinking when I bought these." He frowned at the pair of leather pants he had bought two years ago and never worn.

"Toss them in the give-out pile," I instructed, knowing Miguel would probably burn them. "I don't know why it's taking you forever to pack," I added.

In less than an hour, I had decided which of my belongings I would either give away to Miguel, trash, or take along with me. I had fewer possessions than Fernando did, seeing as my parents weren't well off, and I didn't have a generous uncle who helped me out. Still, it was taking him forever.

"Should I give all the books away?"

"Give them to me," I signed, my eagerness showing. Fernando had a vast collection of books, mostly mystery and thrillers. He often lost interest in them after reading them once, and then would pass them to me. I had no shame when it came to books.

Fernando gave me a sly look. "I gave you one, but you rejected it."

"I'll cause you physical pain," I gestured, warning him. Fernando chuckled at my threat. It was then that Gordo decided he had deprived us of his presence long enough. He leaped off the sill, hopped over the pile, and settled himself in Fernando's lap.

"Lunchtime," Fernando sang.

"That devil just had lunch," I protested.

"Gordo is allowed to have as many meals as he wants." Fernando picked the cat off his lap and stood up. "Do you want a sandwich?"

"Sure," I signed. "I'll come along, so your cat doesn't wheeze over my food."

Fernando shook his head at me to say I was ridiculous. Ridiculous or not, the cat didn't like me, and I didn't trust him.

"When will you be leaving?" Fernando asked after placing Gordo on the counter.

"In a week," I gestured.

"Same," he said. "I'm making a cheese sandwich," Fernando informed me before turning his back to start the preparation.

I allowed myself to savor this moment knowing that in a week, we wouldn't see each other again for months, both of us leading new lives. I accepted the plate of sandwiches from Fernando and practically inhaled mine.

"Should we go to the bowling alley?" Fernando asked.

"After you finish sorting the rest of your stuff?" I wanted to know.

"It's getting boring. We'll do that later. Let's go down to the bowling alley and maybe get drunk later."

"Nobody will sell us alcohol," I reminded him.

"I know where my uncle stashes his vodka."

I shook my head, vehemently rejecting the idea before he finished. Fernando laughed.

"I was joking. But seriously, we have a week to have all the fun we can before we go to separate colleges and carry on with the fun there."

"You mean study, don't you?"

"That too. What do you say? We'll break into my uncle's stash. I'm sure he wouldn't mind a few missing bottles. Come on, Diego," he coaxed. "A few drinks won't automatically turn you into a drunk. You're going to be seventeen soon and we might not be able to celebrate our next birthdays together."

I didn't need to think about it, and because of how eager he was to hear my response, I quickly gave it to him. "Fine."

CHAPTER 13

"So, you're like what—seventeen?" That was the first question my roommate asked me. He was putting up Los Angeles Rams posters on his side of the room above his bed. He turned to me and pushed his hand through his long, wavy hair before he asked me.

I nodded. I had turned seventeen the week before. David cocked his head at me, a thoughtful expression on his face.

"You know, when I was seventeen, I was doing so badly, I thought I was going to be held back. Thank God for those weird brainy kids." He seemed to realize what he had just said, and his expression became sheepish. "Not that I think you're weird or anything. If you are, that's totally cool with me. Weird is fine. I'm rambling. I'll just stop talking." He did and sat cross-legged on his bed, running his hand through his hair, tousling it. "You're Diego Herrera, right? I'm David, David McCarthy. A pleasure to meet you."

I nodded at him and signed I felt the same way. I experienced a lightness in my chest when I saw he understood what the signs I was making meant. It had been a source of anxiety for me, thinking of who I was going to have as a roommate. Margarita had told me tales of horrible roommates, some who were creepy, and others who were distant. The undesirable ones were noisy, dirty, and probably bullies. I often had nightmares about who my roommate would be, and I was glad it was David.

David was cool, but not in the pop culture way. I could call him a hippie, for lack of a better term. David was the only son of two media moguls who wanted him to be the next Mark Zuckerberg. But David wanted something different. He wanted to study music, which had gotten him disowned by his parents. His wealthy grandfather rooted for him, and he had gotten what he wanted.

"They also wanted me to cut my hair. To give up playing the guitar and collecting bobbleheads," David said, gesturing to the shelf where his collection of bobbleheads grinned fixedly at me. He switched them every Tuesday and Saturday at 9:00 a.m. without fail, even when he was late for class. David also folded his clothes into slim rectangles. He had the habit of placing his shoes in a straight line, and he cut his hair once a month by himself. He had never been to the gym, and from the age of ten, he stopped eating meat, fish, and eggs.

"I'm a vegetarian," he told me with a proud beam. "I'm also a Buddhist. 'Bout the only thing my parents tolerate about me."

He told me his grandfather was an ex-judge and traveled a lot after he had retired, often taking him along. David took a gap year, and they both toured Asia, where he discovered Buddhism. David told his tales in a way that didn't make him seem vain or arrogant, and I liked him for that, even if he preferred football to soccer and got preachy whenever I had a hamburger. He had taken several classes on sign language when he learned from the Dean of Student Affairs that I was going to be his roommate.

Leslie, from my Introduction to Literature: Fiction class, apparently had an ongoing history with him. I had no idea if they were dating or just friends, and I hadn't bothered asking. David often went into a long-winded speech about labels and his distaste for them. I didn't know if I agreed with him.

David and Leslie kind of adopted me in my first year in college. David was the cool hippie dad who was chill with everything while Leslie was the snarky mom. They bickered a lot, disagreeing with the other's opinion, and even though I was caught in the middle most of the time, I had fun hanging out with them. They showed me around campus, bringing me to places I could go to if I wanted to be alone, the best eating spots, and the areas to avoid if I didn't want to be harassed by fanatics trolling for the unwary.

It had been Leslie who had come to my rescue after I was pranked by some guys on the campus. That was how we first met. They had given me the wrong directions to the auditorium, where my first class for the semester had been taking place.

"Jerks!" She shook her fist in their direction as they laughed at the joke they had made at my expense. "Come on, kid." That had become her moniker for me: kid. According to her, I looked like I was five. I vehemently disagreed, but it didn't matter to her.

"Why are you looking at my lips like that?" she asked, stopping midway in explaining where the chemistry lab was. Getting the vibe of déjà vu, I stepped back to avoid getting a slap to the face. "Oh!" she exclaimed, realizing. "I wondered why you are so quiet. Most of the dudes I know like to talk. Nerves, I guess. You must be Diego, David's roommate. He told me about you. I'm Leslie Benzenberg-Villareal. There's no need to write when you want to communicate with me. I know a bit of sign language. David is teaching me. I think he planned to introduce us soon. It's a shame his plan is ruined now."

Leslie was tall, thin, and sharp as a whip, and because of her flaming red hair, they called her the scarlet witch. She was half

German, half Latina, and was born in England until her family moved to the United States when she was five. Leslie was the most contradictory person I had ever met. She questioned everything and everyone she saw, continually asking why, even if it was a choice as simple as ordering sashimi instead of sushi. And like David, she hated labels—or boxes, as she called them. It was easy to see why they were friends. David was calm and easygoing, while Leslie was everywhere. It was easy to see how opposites attract.

My first day of college went more or less smooth because of Leslie, although there were a few hiccups. One in the name of Mark Hathaway, a scrawny looking boy in my World Literature class. I had taken the only empty seat in the classroom before the teacher arrived, only for him to kick my chair and tell me to move so he could see. Leslie retorted on my behalf, saying if he really wanted to see what was going on, he wouldn't have chosen to sit at the back of the class.

"Ignore him. He's an idiot," she said, winking at me.

I don't know if it was her comment that made Mark mad, but from then on, he tried his best to make my life miserable in class. He made snide remarks I couldn't hear to other students and tried to trip me when we were outside of the classroom. It made me wonder if we were somehow back in high school. At times, Mark referred to my disabilities, saying his insults to my face. "It's so easy, even a deaf and dumb guy would know," he would always say. He had many reasons to frown. I was beginning to worry those folds would become permanent. Other times, he talked dirt about Mexicans and people of Latino descent.

"After the blacks, they're next. They're always whining and complaining about unfair treatment. They've never done an honest day's work in their lives," he would sneer. "Most of them snuck in. Then they fill up the country with more junkies and dumpster babies. But hey, at least my toilet is clean because of Diego's mom!" he raised his voice to add.

Miles gave him a black eye for that remark. He was half black, half Latino, so he had felt doubly offended by Mark's words.

"Jerk," Miles intoned as Mark tried to get himself up from the floor.

"You hit me!" He was stunned anyone actually would, and I took a grim sort of pleasure at the sight of him.

"Yes, he did, and I'll give you a broken nose to match if you don't shut it!" Leslie growled at him. "Good job, Miles," she high-fived him.

When Mr. Benedict asked what had happened to his eye, he lied. Perhaps he feared rebuttal if he snitched, so he gave an unconvincing tale of slamming his face into a door. Mr. Benedict gave a skeptical look before he moved on.

I had thought Mark was all bark and no bite, and Miles' punch had taken most from him, but I was wrong. When I woke the next morning for class, I found my car vandalized with "Go back to Mexico, Wetback!" spray-painted on the hood and sides. My skin had turned red with anger. It was only because of David's intervention that I didn't march to his hall and give him another black eye and a broken nose to match. The bigotry and discrimination to which I had been subjected since my childhood had grown tiresome.

"It isn't worth the fight, Diego, trust me. I'll help you fix it. A friend of mine owns a garage. He's a great painter. Don't worry about it, and don't think about paying. Think of it as an early birthday gift or Christmas or something."

The car would cost hundreds of dollars to fix, but I didn't want to get into an argument with him—not while I was running late for class. I gave him an energetic thumbs-up and smiled.

"I agree. Something has to be done about Mark before he decides to break your legs. I think it would be something of a joke to him, something about lame, mute, and deaf. He is that vicious, so stay with Leslie and Miles," he warned with a serious look on his face.

Mark did make the lame, mute, and deaf joke, but no one laughed at it, and he didn't seem to care. His high spirits bothered and infuriated me, but I kept my cool. During class, Mark tapped me insistently on the shoulder and mimed falling down the stairs before mouthing, "I'm going to get you." I was so afraid he would act on his threat that I stuck with Leslie and only left her when I absolutely had to. I was always on my guard. I didn't sleep well that night, and my nerves were frayed the following morning, only to discover Mark wasn't in his usual spot.

"I heard he was called to the dean's office," Miles wrote to me when Mr. Benedict's back was turned.

Mark himself wasn't there to dispute that. He wasn't in class the next day or the day after that. After two weeks of absence, I could finally relax. A month later, I heard he had been "advised" to try another college. At whose behest, I had wondered.

"David's, dude," Fernando had told me after I had texted him about what was going on. "I googled his parents and his grandfather. They have enough clout to convince puny Mark to move if he knows what's best for him. I'm so jealous of you, Diego. All I've got here is a roommate who talks all day long about jazz music and girls who are addicted to Tic Tacs. I've heard more about the rise of jazz than I care to in my lifetime."

I didn't tell Mom what was happening in school. It wasn't as if she could help me. Oregon was way out of her reach, and the best she could do was try to comfort me and fret about how I was coping, which I knew she was doing already.

David never told me if he had anything to do with Mark, and I never bothered trying to ask, knowing I would just get his blank look again.

In my other classes, I was basically left alone. Leslie was also in my Introduction to Classical Literature class, and we threw paper planes discretely at each other. In the other courses, I was on my own, and no one talked to me unless it was essential. A girl, Brenda, tried to ask me out. In her words, she wanted to see if we could revise the subject material over coffee. I was so taken aback by the suddenness, I said no before I could think it over.

David had laughed himself silly when I told him. It didn't help matters when Leslie arrived in the evening and informed me Brenda was crying from embarrassment. Her roommates were amused that a guy like me didn't think she was all right to go out with.

"No offense," Leslie added.

There was none taken. I was still trying to wrap my head around the fact that I just made someone a laughing stock. How many people had been watching when she asked me?

"It's not your fault, Diego," Leslie tried to comfort me. "She caught you off guard."

I tried apologizing to Brenda the next day, but she marched off with her nose in the air, and about two weeks later, Leslie told me she was dating Jake from her College Composition 1 class.

"She's nothing to cry over, believe me. The two of you wouldn't have lasted a month."

Not that I was looking for a girlfriend—the memory of

Seema was still pretty fresh. But I was glad Brenda had moved on. She appeared to be so happy in her relationship that she had forgotten to be angry with me and gave me a wave anytime I entered class. I was always glad to reciprocate the gesture.

College was basically easy from then on. I attended classes regularly and distinguished myself as a diligent student who steadily got A's and who hung out with David McCarthy, Leslie Benzenberg-Villareal, and Miles Marquina.

After Brenda, another girl asked me out, and I said yes, not wanting to embarrass her or get laughed at by David. It was a particularly weird date. She kept staring into my eyes and complementing the color before drifting into a conversation about her dad's hunting trophies. That was thankfully the first and last date we ever went on. Perhaps she saw I wasn't interested and moved on, or she didn't find me as attractive as she had hoped. There were no hard feelings, but David did laugh at me and called me a lady killer. I flung a pillow at him.

CHAPTER 14

"Have you ever been to a party before?" Tommy asked. He was one of David's acquaintances. When I had prodded him about it, he'd given me a cryptic comment about people who needed his positive vibe and continued cutting his hair. I never asked him again.

I didn't like Tommy, and he had the same feeling of immense dislike for me. Leslie wasn't fond of him either but said she respected David's decision to have him as a hanger on. He had called me a freak the first time we met before proceeding to plonk his muddy boots on David's study desk and put a bobblehead out of place. That had cemented my dislike for him. He always pushed and prodded David, trying to see if he would finally make him react violently, but David never did. He never yelled or showed his anger; he was calm about everything Tommy did. So, bored, he turned his attention to me.

Unlike David, I could ignore him by simply presenting my back to him and pretend he wasn't there, which infuriated him. There was nothing Tommy loved more than being the center of attention. However, there was nothing he could do about my decision to ignore him. So, Tommy saved the vitriol for when I could read his lips. He wasn't any worse than Sebastian or Mark; it was the same old insult.

149

"What? They're letting babies still in diapers attend school now!" That had been the second thing he'd said after he saw me. "Freakish baby," he chuckled.

"Leave him alone, man," David said, coming to my defense.

I turned my back to him just as he was about to deliver a scathing reply. His mocking wasn't particularly creative—just the same things I had heard all my life. Same old, same old about my being Mexican and the stereotype about being smuggled in, my mom being a housecleaner, and, finally, my disabilities.

Leslie told me to leave the room whenever he came around, but I detested the idea of leaving my room because he was there. Turning my back to him was an efficient and straightforward tactic; it was my way of dismissing him.

He didn't tease Leslie whenever she was around. Instead, he flirted with her—or tried to because she instantly shut him down. I guessed there was a history between them, but I never asked for clarity. I had a feeling Leslie would thump me if I did. She could be scary at times.

I was glad when I joined the college's soccer team, and our practice time was slated during the hours Tommy made his visits. We had practice four times a week, and that was four times less that I had to see Tommy's mug in my week. Hallelujah. I was surprised to learn Tommy's cousin, Brayden, was on the team, and he wasn't a jerk like his relative. He was pretty much like David but not entirely—no one could be like David, and he laughed easily. He was the captain of the team and made me feel welcomed.

The college soccer team wasn't like my former high school team. Not all the members were enthusiastic like the coach was about my presence in the group. At worst, they were indifferent. As long as I didn't jeopardize the game, they had nothing against me. Yet no matter what I did or no matter how the coach marveled about my raw talent and potential, they never lost the skeptical look on their faces. One day, I would win them over.

It was weird having a coach who was delighted with what I could do. Coach Miller never acknowledged I was a prodigy on the field. He would only give a curt nod whenever I did something right. The next time we practiced, Coach Miller expected me to repeat it without slipping. Coach Shaw was supportive, and at first, it niggled at me that he praised each and every one of us so effusively, especially me. Still, I grew used to it, although I preferred Coach Miller's form of coaching.

Brayden never spoke to me outside of the team. In his defense, he was a year above me and stayed off campus, so we never ran into each other. I wished it could be like that with Tommy.

It was Sunday, and we had practice in the morning, but the coach ended the session early when it began to rain. I ran back to my dorm, wet and muddy, thinking about how Coach Miller would have had us continue even if it were raining fire and brimstone. Coach Shaw was a breath of fresh air. I'd bounded into the room to see Tommy reclined on David's bed. David was sitting on the edge of my bed, tuning his guitar.

"Hey!" he yelled when he saw me dripping all over the place. "I just cleaned the floors!"

He only stopped scowling after I cleaned up and moved from my bed to his chair to make room for me. It was then Tommy made an invitation.

It was surprising he was talking to me without his usual jeer until I pondered on the question and saw the hidden barb. I nodded yes, wary, and watchful for traps.

"There's a sorority party tonight if you'd like to come. The Thetas are having their annual whatchamacallit thingy tonight.

It'll be fun… if you don't mind parties."

His offer surprised me, and I looked to David to see what he made of this. He was looking at Tommy with a thoughtful expression on his face. *Why not?* I thought. I'd never been to a college party, and I heard they were wilder and even more fun than a high school party. Fernando had been to one and had nothing but glowing reports, both of which surprised me. If Tommy were offering, it would be rude to turn down his peace offering—if it was one and not an elaborate scheme to humiliate me.

David turned to me with his brows raised as if to say: *what's your answer?*

"I guess," I signed, and his face darkened to a scowl.

"What did he say?" Tommy asked.

"He's not going," David said shortly.

"Is that your answer or his?"

"Diego has that report to type for Dr. Sinclair's class."

I'd already finished my assignment on Friday. I wondered why he was lying.

"Chill out, mom," Tommy drawled, rolling his eyes. "He'll be back before bedtime, and he can take care of himself, despite his condition," he sneered. I was pumped about the idea of the party, so I didn't really mind.

"You in?" he asked directly, and I nodded. "Cool, I'll pick you up by eight. Wear something cool. Later, David." He strode out the door, and I was left with David.

"Do you think that was stupid of me?" I inquired.

David put his guitar aside before answering me. "No, why would you think that?"

"You didn't want me to go to the party."

"Oh, great Gandhi, no! I didn't want you to go with Tommy. Or go to the party."

"Why?"

"Because the Theta girls are kinda mean. The 'B' word gets tossed around a lot when people refer to them. They're kinda like Tommy, but female and louder."

"So, I shouldn't go?" I gestured.

"Dear Buddha, no. You should. I mean, it's an experience, part of the culture of our great college."

"So, you'll come with me?" I wanted to know.

"No."

"You should go with him, David," Leslie said as she picked out clothes for me to wear, ignoring my protests that just jeans and a t-shirt would be fine. She had gone through my things and was now rifling through David's for something she deemed suitable enough for me to wear.

"No." David adamantly shook his head.

"Not even if the entire world decides to practice Ahimsa," Leslie probed.

"Not even for that," David said grimly.

"Liar. What about this jacket?"

I held my hands up to my face and cringed in horror. Even David winced at the monstrosity he had in his closet.

"You both are idiots," she said, tossing the jacket at David. "If you weren't going to wear it, why did you buy a rock star jacket?"

"It was a birthday gift from a cousin in Sienna. I guess she thinks Americans dress flashy. Please put it back. And as for following Diego to the party, he made his bed, so he should be prepared for Procrustes to either stretch him until he fits into it or chop off his overhanging limbs. Whichever."

"That's not the saying," Leslie protested.

"Not making me feel better," I also protested.

"That's not my job," he responded.

I threw a pillow at him.

Leslie ended up picking a pair of distressed jeans, a shirt, and an artfully battered leather jacket—a slight variation of what I had suggested wearing in the first place.

"Knock 'em dead," Leslie said, giving me a thumbs-up.

The party almost knocked me dead. Sometimes I forgot the reason why I didn't like going to parties. My hearing aids basically amplified sounds. The pop music blaring from the speaker was doubly amplified. My head was aching, and I hadn't even been in the place for five minutes.

The Theta house was built to imitate a Greek temple and an old Victorian statehouse. Just when I started regretting coming, Tommy abandoned me and went off with a blond girl. I was left alone with a splitting headache, lamenting my decision. I should have stayed in my room and studied instead. I was considering leaving without telling Tommy when someone tapped my shoulder, and I looked around to see a petite girl smiling at me. I smiled back, wondering if I knew her.

"Diego, right? I'm Lucy," she introduced herself, smiling. "I sit behind you in Introduction to Literature: Poetry. Seems like this is going to be an unforgettable night!"

The lighting was dim, so I couldn't read her lips properly and filled in most of the gaps myself. I was unable to understand what she said next, but she took my hand in hers and began towing me through the crowd of partiers as they danced, all the way to the kitchen where she poured us both some drinks.

She might have asked if I preferred vodka, but I wasn't so sure with the dimness and my headache. I took a sip of the beer she had served me and hoped that was enough of an answer to whatever question she'd posed.

We stood by the beer kegs, quietly sipping from our cups until she started jumping up and down. I got the feeling she was saying something, but I couldn't see, and that made me feel even more lost and helpless. I needed to get out of there. Lucy hastily grabbed the cup from my hand and set hers and mine down on the table and dragged me to the dance floor. The sound changed to something more profound, and she danced as though the DJ was playing her favorite music.

I did my absolute best to keep up with her moves, but it wasn't enough. I was exhausted and longed for the warmth and silence of my dorm. To my relief, she took my hand once again to drag me off the dance floor, mercifully leading me outside where the noise levels were much more tolerable. Though it was dark, which was just as unnerving, as I couldn't see her. Seconds later, I felt hands touch my shoulders, moving up to my neck, and then there was something wet on my chin. Thoroughly creeped out, I tore myself away, only to realize it was her—Lucy had been trying to kiss me!

I heard her shout. I couldn't hear the words, but I felt her hands connect with my chest, pushing me back. She did it again and again, angrily. My temper was beginning to rise too. When she pushed at me again, I slapped her hands away, stormed back into the house, thrust past the partygoers, and walked out the door.

I was still shaking with anger as I strode back to my dorm, blaming Tommy for what had happened. It might not have been his fault, but he was a convenient person to blame. It was no secret that he hated me. He might have deliberately invited me to the party then abandoned me so I'd make a fool of myself. A deaf guy who is unable to speak in a place with dim lighting—why! Anyone could accuse him of anything, and he wouldn't be able to defend himself.

"You're back early," David noted, looking up from his book when I stalked into the room, slamming the door behind me.

"How astute of you!" I signed.

He looked at me with a cocked eyebrow. "You've only been gone for an hour. What happened?"

I ignored him, pulling my shoes, and then shrugging out of the jacket. I looked at David. He had closed his textbook, and his eyes were fixated on me.

"Did Tommy do something to you?"

I didn't answer, but my anger was draining away, leaving me feeling exhausted.

"He left you alone, didn't he?"

I nodded before signing, "And then got mauled by a crazy girl. I think I'll have nightmares for the rest of my life. You should have seen her come at me!"

It was good to see David laugh; it helped brighten my spirits.

"I figured you'd have a headache when you returned, so I left out some ibuprofen in case you need it. Leslie left you a hamburger."

I signed my thanks, took the pills, and devoured the hamburger.

"I'm curious about this girl who pushed you around. What does she look like?"

"I can't even say. I know the girl is petite and her name is Lucy. Is she a Theta girl?" I gestured.

David spread his hands. "How should I know? You look exhausted. Get some sleep. I'll hear this wonderful story another day."

I fell asleep as soon as my head hit the pillow. In class the next day, I looked out for Lucy to apologize but didn't see her anywhere. People looked at me weird, though. They would send surreptitious glances my way and then pretend not to when they saw me glancing in their direction. It was awkward and worrisome. I wondered what kind of sick and twisted pleasure could someone derive from trying to hurt others and make their lives miserable just because they are different. I asked myself if the bullying would ever come to an end.

It turned out the incident between Lucy and I hadn't been as private as I thought. Someone actually caught it on video. Leslie told me Lucy called me names that would have made my ears burn. She asked if I was okay with people hollering at me, and I shrugged. I treated them like I did Tommy—I just turned my back to them.

CHAPTER 15

"Are you still interested in a part-time job?" Leslie asked me, pouring more ketchup onto her stash of fries. We had crashed David's solo fries time. Now, he was tolerating our presence by keeping silent and glowering at Leslie, who kept stealing his fries, even though hers were right in front of her. She was boring David to tears while I was attempting to finish my assignment.

"Yeah," I signed. Leslie was quickly learning sign language from David and didn't often need to glance at him to provide an interpretation.

"Good. There's an opening for a server at Sunshine Café, just off campus, and they pay 10.75 an hour plus tips. The owner, Mr. Gibson, understands a bit of sign language, which would help make the communication easier between you two. Is this something that would interest you?"

"Sure," I gestured, excited, and grateful she had fulfilled her promise. I had mentioned getting a part-time job weeks ago, but I wasn't sure how to start looking. Leslie had promised to help me search for one with decent pay.

"Sunshine Café." David was finally coming out of his self-imposed silence. "Isn't that where Cathy works?"

"Used to. Cathy quit yesterday. That's why there's an opening. What do you say, Diego?"

"Isn't the owner, like, an ogre? He drove Cathy to tears like five times a day. Isn't that why she quit?"

Leslie flapped her hand as if to say his concerns were unwarranted. "Cathy cries at the drop of a hat, and Diego is made of stronger stuff. What do you say, Diego?"

"Don't do it, Diego," David warned me. "It isn't worth it."

"Sometimes, customers leave excellent tips," Leslie said.

"It wouldn't hurt to try," I gestured to David, lifting my shoulders. I really needed the extra cash. Every time I texted home for pocket money, I felt beyond guilty.

"Yes!" Leslie exclaimed. "The kid has spoken. I've spoken to Mr. Gibson, and he's expecting you by three. I fixed it so it won't clash with your soccer practice. Your shift would be from three to five every day except for Sundays. Best of all, it's close to campus. Is that okay with you?"

I nodded, not knowing what to say but grateful nonetheless.

"Good, when you get there, just tell him Leslie sent you. I've told him about you, but be careful. He is an ogre just like David said, but only because he's particular about certain things being done a certain way. So, be sure to follow his rules by the letter. He is a stickler for rules, and he also has a strict dress code. That's why I thought you'd be perfect for the job, Diego," she concluded, beaming proudly.

"Because he's good at taking orders?" David asked.

"No, because he dresses like your dad, and that would really impress Gibson."

David did not argue against that and turned to me with a serious look on his face.

"Gibson has no soft, mushy exterior. He is full-on evil and enjoys terrorizing his employees and customers. He will break you, and believe me when I say it's better to live the rest of your life without knowing what that feels like. He won't stand for any sass, any spunk, or anything that makes life worth living. Sometimes I wonder why he opened the café if he's so bitter over life."

Leslie tapped my hand, bringing my attention to her. "Ignore Rambling Rosie here." She jerked her thumb in David's direction. "Sure, Gibson is gruff and a perfectionist—and maybe a tad sardonic—but he's a solid guy, and if you don't give him any cause to, he won't chew you up and spit you out."

Henry Gibson, the owner of Sunshine café, was a stocky man with a mop of curly, brown hair. He had penetrating blue eyes that shone vividly against his tanned skin. From what I had gathered from Leslie and David, I assumed Gibson was middle-aged. To my surprise, he looked in his late twenties, and he wasn't an ogre. As Leslie said he would be, Gibson was gruff, and he did have a thing about everything being in its proper place. Apart from that, he was almost pleasant. He was just like David whenever he encountered dirt or a fork put out of place.

"Leslie told me you can't speak or hear," he signed to me when I arrived at five minutes to three. He was stern about punctuality as well, and I wanted to score a point by arriving earlier.

I nodded.

"My sign language is quite rusty. I only studied it for a short time when I was a freshman in college. Leslie mentioned you understand how to read lips, which is fantastic, so I'm going to speak instead. As for the job, it doesn't require you to talk much. Although that's what *these ones* specialize in—talking the day away," he said, pointing to a couple of workers in the kitchen. "You know what a server's work entails, right? You take the customers' orders, bring their orders to them, and then clear the table once they are done. I pay you 10.75 dollars an hour, and you keep any tips."

I nodded.

"As for the dress code, I expect my employees to maintain a clean appearance, which means no scruffiness and whatever else might constitute as uncleanliness. Number two: no dating among my employees. I had a couple a few years back, and their drama almost cost me the café. Number three: punctuality. Your shift starts at three, which means I expect you to be here ten minutes prior. If you're going to be late, I'd like at least a two-hour heads-up, accompanied by a reasonable excuse. Number four: you must always be polite and courteous to whoever comes in here. Even if they are the most obnoxious people you've ever had the misfortune to come across. If they're behaving in their obnoxious way, don't get into an argument with them. I personally handle kicking out stupid customers that's my job. Yours is serving them. Got all that?"

I nodded.

"Good. Let's begin."

I was given a one-week trial. If I made a mistake at any point during that probationary period, I was out. No amount of apology and begging would make Gibson give me another opportunity. I did my best to be extra careful not to commit the slightest fault, although there were trying times.

Some of the customers were obnoxious, as Gibson had forewarned. They changed their minds frequently. Some took longer to decide what they wanted, so I paid close attention to their lips to jot down their orders when they were ready. Others noticed my disability and thought that speaking louder and slower would help me hear them better. This was exasperating and made me feel frustrated. One made an unfunny joke about monkeys serving at the café, and before I could do anything, Gibson materialized out from nowhere and escorted them out. He had a way of doing that, just slightly gliding up to you when you least expected, so one always had to be on their toes.

On the last day of my trial period, I had the pleasure of serving a particularly obnoxious woman. She wanted to bring her dog inside with her despite the glaringly obvious "no pets allowed" signs placed everywhere.

"I said Macy is eating with me, are you deaf?" she demanded in a shrill tone.

I was puffed up with so much indignation I was almost afraid I'd burst. "Are you blind? Can you not see the signs?" I retorted, signing furiously.

Her face had gone red with rage. Clearly, by her reaction, she wasn't used to being told no.

"What was that? What did you just do with your fingers?" She rose to her feet; her Yorkshire Terrier tucked under her arm. I could feel all the other customers' eyes swivel toward us, ready to watch the drama unfold.

Gibson suddenly materialized beside me.

"Is everything all right here?" he inquired calmly.

"No!" the woman screamed. "This waiter of yours signed something foul at me!"

I glared at the woman for her blatant lie before turning to look at Gibson. He raised his eyebrow at me.

"I see. Diego, please repeat the sign for me."

I did as he asked.

"There!" the woman yelled. "That's the sign."

I trembled with rage.

"I'm afraid that isn't a foul sign, ma'am. He's just explaining we don't allow pets in here, no matter how precious they are. We have rules at the café that all clients must abide to. If you want to—"

"Macy," the woman supplied.

Gibson gave her a gentle smile. "If you want to eat with Macy, I'm afraid you're going to have to do it elsewhere. Try the crab restaurant down the street."

"I don't want crab!"

Gibson's frame moved before me, cutting off my view of her. I took that as my cue to leave, so I returned to the kitchen. Later, I learned he threatened to call the cops. That's what had finally made her leave, but not before she told Gibson he'd be sorry for his actions.

Turned out the woman was Rachel Young, a food blogger, and she wrote a horrific review about Sunshine Café. The five of us huddled around Maggie's phone and read her accusations of terrible service and terrible food. Gibson did his creeping up on people act and scared the hell out of us, but he forgot to reprimand us when he saw the article. It was the first time I saw him laugh, and it made him seem younger.

"Back to work, everyone," he ordered with a smile. "And Maggie, phone in the locker." With a preoccupied face, she nodded yes and quickly stored it away.

Four other employees worked the same hours as me. Maggie worked in the café as a waitress. She had a love for gossip and sold hair products on the side. Mario was a barista and a conspiracy theorist. He had a YouTube channel where he explored the possibilities of Michael Jackson being alive and where Atlantis sunk. Ted mopped the floors and cleaned up the messes. He was the only son of an African American and a second-generation Korean. He was majoring in English Literature and planned to visit his roots after college. His dreams made me think about Mexico. Mom, Dad, and Margarita could never return, but I could, along with Miguel. We could go to Ixtepec and see the home Mom grew up in.

When I got my first paycheck, I really had no need for money. So, I halved it and sent a part home, glowing with a positive feeling as I did so.

I was woken on a slightly cloudy Saturday morning by my phone vibrating beneath the pillow. David and I had stayed awake almost the entire night watching movies on his laptop. I couldn't recall when I'd dragged myself to bed, but I woke to find myself there, covered up to my chin with my blanket.

Feeling hot, I kicked the blanket off and yawned excessively before checking my phone. I had fourteen messages from Miguel. I immediately sprung up, my heart thumping so loudly I thought it would stop. I opened one, and its contents made me hope that I was still asleep and just having a bad nightmare.

Mom and Dad have been arrested!

There was a faint throbbing at the back of my head, and my mind wandered to today's date. It wasn't April Fools; this couldn't be a prank. Miguel wasn't prone to jokes like this, not after Mom punished him severely for pulling a stunt like that. Miguel still winces when he remembers that day.

I went through all the messages, my heart hammering against my ribcage as a fog of dread swamped me. I had always lived in fear of a day like this—a day when my family was finally caught after years of keeping our heads down and playing it safe. Mom and Dad would be deported, Miguel would be sent to a foster home, and Margarita—I don't know what would happen to her. I didn't even know where she was.

I was scared and frustrated; I couldn't call them and offer the comfort of my voice, I had to communicate with them through text. Sacramento was a seven-hour drive away. I could get there before nightfall if I drove without a break.

Miguel, what happened?

His reply was immediate. From the abbreviations and misspellings in his text messages, I got that two detectives had called, something else about a Raquel and a Mike, and they had taken them down to the station to identify something. Mom had asked Miguel to stay back and watch the house and to call Fernando's uncle, Guillermo, to tell him to stay put at home. Miguel was scared and texted me, asking me what he should do. I told him to stay at home.

It seemed our parents hadn't been arrested as Miguel had feared, but they were close to being found out. Anything could happen, and the authorities could have them arrested and deported. This was the worst nightmare that could happen to an undocumented immigrant family. The thought of being round up and treated like a criminal, innocent children separated from their parents, their friends, and their loved ones, and from the only life they have ever known, to be sent to a country they have never known where their lives could be put at danger. I shuddered at the thought.

I went through my older messages and emails to see if Mom had left me a message; there was one from Guillermo telling me under no circumstance was I to leave school. My heart returned to my chest when I confirmed Mom and Dad hadn't been arrested; there was some dead body, and the police thought my parents might be able to identify it. After some routine questioning, they would be back home as if nothing had happened. I prayed that would be the case.

Leslie, David, and I had planned to see a basketball game.

Knowing in my frame of mind that I would be a sour puss, I pleaded upset stomach and asked them to leave so I could stew in peace. It was then I remembered the saying, "A problem shared is a problem half-solved." I could tell David about the troubles at home, but something stopped me. I felt I would be making a monumental mistake by confiding in an outsider about something that had been my family's secret for years. So, I smiled through my pretend pain and told them to have fun.

I must have dozed off as I waited for Guillermo's message. The vibrations of a new message woke me, and my heart lifted when I saw it was from Mom. She informed me they were okay and back home, telling me not to worry.

It was easier said than done. While I was relieved my parents were safe at home, I was still concerned over Mom and Dad's close encounter with the police. I was scared something like that would reoccur, and there would be no coming back home for them.

Whose body were you asked to identify?

Mike's. Margarita's boyfriend. I think Margarita is in deep trouble, Diego. We have absolutely no idea where she is, and we are worried sick. Mike was shot and killed while robbing a gas station. When the police came, he tried to shoot, and he was shot instead. They said there was another person with him, a girl, but she got away in a car, and now they're looking for her. We don't know if the girl was your sister or someone else. They hurt people, Dieguito, and one of them was a little girl. They found a letter addressed to us. That's why we were asked to identify the body. We told them he was Margarita's boyfriend; maybe that's why the message was in his pocket. When they asked, we informed them she had broken up with Mike a long time ago. Oh, my Dieguito, I don't know what to do.

I knew what the next course of action was—cut Margarita off entirely before we ended up paying for her sins. I was glad it was over, but I was beyond furious at Margarita. After I was done texting Mom, I sent quite a scathing message to Margarita and ended it by asking her never to call. Even as I did so, I was worried about her. If she was the girl the cops were after, then they would be pressing charges when they caught her. *One of them was a little girl.* How high had she been when she and Mike attempted the robbery? I imagined her in a dark room, sobbing with remorse and regret. But I couldn't take back the message, and frankly, I didn't want to.

When David and Leslie returned, I was in a better mood and tried to put Margarita out of my mind.

CHAPTER 16

"Could I have another cup of coffee?" Rebecca asked. She was one of the regulars, and one of the few Gibson had a genuine smile for. Like Gibson, Rebecca had a calm way of speaking, but hers wasn't so deadpan. She also smiled more often and sometimes wore flowers in her hair, tucked behind her left ear, and always had something red or yellow as part of her outfit.

Today, it was a butter yellow beanie, and the rose was tucked into her shirt's pocket. She was smiling as usual, but her mood was a bit dim.

"Are you all right?" I asked her. She understood sign language, and we often conversed using just that when I was supposed to be on my break.

She was an architecture student and a freshman like me. Our paths hardly crossed in school except for the night at a bonfire. Leslie had insisted I come along since it was a university tradition and experience. Rebecca hung out with us that night.

"I'm fine, just a little headache. Hey, Diego, there's an art exhibit at Kathy Williams' gallery tomorrow evening. Wanna come along with me?"

Tomorrow was Sunday, and I had nothing to do after practice. David and I planned to snooze through the day and maybe go out for some Chinese food later in the evening.

"Sure," I gestured, and she smiled brightly at me.

"I think Diego has been on more dates this semester than I have my entire life!" David was complaining to Leslie, as she once again appointed herself as my personal stylist.

"That's because you're preachy, David dear, and Diego here has—"

"Don't say animal magnetism," David cut in before Leslie could finish her statement.

She scowled in his direction. "I was going to say he has a strong, silent personality."

"I thought girls dig the mysterious fella," David said.

"Have you ever seen anyone more mysterious than the quiet type?" Leslie asked him.

David grumbled something unintelligible.

"Just play it cool, Diego," Leslie told me. I remembered Margarita giving me advice for my first date with Seema. I felt my stomach clench as I remembered where our relationship had ended. I was no longer replying to Margarita's texts. It seemed like years ago when that had taken place instead of a few months ago.

"We're just going as friends," I informed her.

David and Leslie snorted at my naïveté.

"Yeah, because 'friends' hang out at the art gallery," David said, air quoting the word *friends*. "If she wanted to hang as friends, it would be pizza, soda, and painting toenails."

My face crumpled in a grimace of distaste. "Is that what the two of you are up to whenever I'm not around?" I signed.

They shrugged their shoulders.

"What about a cashmere sweater, paired with slacks, oxfords, and maybe those black hipster glasses?"

"He's not visiting his girlfriend's suburban parents for the first time."

"Overkill," I sided with David, already anxious about what Leslie would finally choose. She told me I was incapable of choosing clothes beyond hoodies and jeans, so I couldn't be trusted to make choices. I didn't dispute her and was content to shoot down most of her options with David's help.

"You two are the worst," she informed us.

Leslie finally decided on a white tee, paired with khaki pants and white sneakers. To finish the whole look, she added a jacket I kept on, and nerd glasses that I rejected.

"Are you picking her up from her dorm, or will you be meeting her at the gallery?" Leslie wanted to know as she brushed off invisible lint from my jacket. "There," she said with a satisfied smile. "You look dapper."

David made a protesting sound. "Nobody," he began with his remonstration, waving his pick, "in our generation uses words such as dapper or the likes."

"Says the dude whose favorite oath is Jiminy Cricket," Leslie returned. "Picking her up or meeting her?" she asked me again.

"Meeting her," I signed, finding my palms were sweaty. I tried not to wipe them on my pants.

"Rebecca is a sweet girl. If this goes off without a hitch, you two just might be going to the Oregon Bach Festival together."

"I don't like your matchmaking scheme," David informed her. "Diego wants to focus on his university education and his budding soccer career. He has no time for dating. And would you please stop fussing over him? He's going to start laying eggs if you don't let him go soon."

I didn't agree with David on the egg-laying part. Although I felt I would cancel or something if I wasn't out of my dorm in five minutes. Leslie did the last of her grooming, and I was finally allowed to leave. My pre-date jitters died a bit as I drove out of campus to 44 East 7th Avenue, where the gallery was.

The art exhibit was a semi-formal affair. People were in tuxedos, evening dresses, and relatively fancy attire. I was glad I let Leslie pick out my clothes even though I felt they were a tad too casual. Rebecca was wearing a yellow knee-length dress that resembled sunflowers, and she had a yellow rose stuck in the messy bun she had piled her hair into.

"I'm glad you came," she smiled at me as we sat on a bench while others mingled in the anteroom. "I honestly thought you were going to cancel."

"Why would you think that?" I gestured.

"I don't know. I just thought you'd bail, that's all."

I didn't know how to respond to that, so I asked instead, "So, do you know the artist?"

"Yeah, he's my crazy uncle. He put everything together in a week and insisted on showing the world as soon as possible. So here we are. I think he included an auction, as well. Oh, it's about to start."

She was right. People had already started drifting in through the open door. Rebecca got up carefully and held out her hand to me. I took it, and we walked hand in hand into the gallery.

Her uncle may be mad, but he was talented. I was in a constant state of awe as I more or less gawked at his paintings and sketches. Most of his works were abstract, and his technique incorporated dark tones around light ones. More than half of the others were surrealist, and the rest were portraits.

"He likes painting on themes of death and life. The continual struggle of the two," she said. "I was the model for that one," she added as she pointed to a very chaotic painting.

It was quite confusing with all the gray wisps swirling about a

171

tiny figure wearing a red dress. The character seemed to be in the process of rising from or sitting on a chair, clinging to a crutch. On closer inspection, I saw that the gray wisps were words, some encouraging, some vindictive and nasty.

"It's unlike the others, the theme is of struggle," Rebecca explained. "There's my uncle."

He didn't look all that crazy, except for his hair, which was sticking out in every direction. He was dressed almost similarly to me but had a lime green pocket square tucked into his jacket. I tried not to notice how it clashed with the neutral colors of the rest of his clothes, but the color's brightness kept drawing my eyes towards it, an effect I guessed was deliberate on his part.

"Arty Blume." His handshake was firm and quick. "You must be Diego. Rebecca told me she was bringing someone. Tell me, Diego, how do you see my work? It's okay, I understand sign language."

"I don't know much about art," I began signing, "but they are fascinating pieces. I like this one best so far."

"Why? Because Rebecca is in it?" he asked with an odd twinkle in his eyes. Rebecca slapped his arm to stop him from continuing.

"No, I mean part of it. But I like it because it depicts the struggle everyone goes through in life with people either being with us or against us. The person in the painting seemed to be caught in a continuous cycle of being pushed down by hateful words and helped up by the kind, encouraging words others have to give. That's why I like it. There is this hopeful look on the figure's face that tells me they hadn't given up yet, and that's admirable."

"Hmm, I like him, Rebecca. Invite him to the fundraiser." He patted Rebecca's shoulder before drifting off. His gait bore a resemblance to Rebecca's.

"Told you he was weird," Rebecca said with a fond light in her eyes. "Do you want to wait for the auction? Or should we get out of here?"

We had only been in the gallery for an hour. While I wasn't bored, I was intimidated by the prices the paintings and sketches were listed under. They were quite beautiful, and it was almost painful knowing I could never possess them.

"Where do you want us to go?" I gestured at her.

"Do you like volunteer work?"

I shrugged. I'd never volunteered for anything unless you could count volunteering to bathe Gordo.

"Would you like to?" Rebecca went on.

"Yeah," I signed back.

That was how I'd come to know the other life of Rebecca Blume.

───────

Rebecca was born with a deficiency called spina bifida. For some people, it was merely a fancy medical name and a disability. For her parents, it had been a source of disappointment, emotions flying about, and ultimately divorce. For Rebecca, it meant a lifetime of discomfort. Since Rebecca was a child, she had been through numerous procedures. They monitored how Rebecca walked, how she ran, and how she was tempted to gaily skip from one stepping stone to another across a stream of water. She wasn't allowed to do that because her parents had feared she would slip and crack her head against a stone. Rebecca did so despite her parents' admonishment, and nothing bad happened to her. She underwent physical therapy sessions for a few hours every day and had come to resent that she would sometimes need crutches or braces to aid her in walking.

All the things Rebecca had gone through had given her tremendous courage, permanently impacting her outlook on life.
Her strength and resilience were admirable, and I could identify
with her on a deep level that I had not with any other person.
The hardship we had both been through gave us the ability to
understand each other. Like me, her suffering had enabled her to
appreciate the essential things in life.

She admitted that it had taken a while before she let go of
the resentment she had felt and realized how fortunate she was.
There were others out there who suffered from the same condition that she did or something different. Most didn't have
wealthy parents like her, who could afford the best help money
could buy, and depended on charitable organizations instead.
After coming to that realization, she decided to stop feeling sorry
for herself and do something for others. That's how she started
her charity work. The love her parents had shown her allowed
her to recognize its importance and the necessity to return that
love to others by helping those who needed it the most. She was
a beautiful and compassionate person, and I felt truly blessed and
privileged to know her.

Her mom had gotten custody of her after the divorce, but
she wasn't always at home. Her uncles, Arty and Josh, practically
raised her. They repeatedly held fundraisers and donated to char-
ities. Their actions had influenced her, but she aspired to do
things differently. Rebecca didn't want to just give money away
at events; she wanted to be hands-on in the lives of others. As a
result, she visited shelters and orphanages and special-needs
schools. She made blankets, cupcakes, told stories and volunteered in every event.

"After classes, I usually have nothing to do, so why not do

the needful?" she told me. "I work with a public foundation, apart from my uncles', and we're currently raising money to help children with Down syndrome."

I donated twenty dollars when she told me about it, and even though that was all the money I had, I felt proud to do so. It was a wonderful feeling to be of help to others who direly needed it.

Rebecca invited me to the fundraiser as we left the gallery for my car. I had to decline because it clashed with my work schedule and soccer practice.

"It's cool. Hey, have you ever been to Crater Lake National Park?"

When I shook my head, she gave a shocked reaction.

"You haven't been there? We'll go together next Sunday. If you don't mind, that is."

I didn't mind. From the smug smile on Leslie's face, she envisioned the second date or hangout. Because of her correct predictions, she wore infuriatingly huge grins and rose her eyebrows insinuatingly for the rest of the week. I didn't mind that either.

Rebecca was refreshing and fun to be with. I felt at peace with her. I didn't have to pretend to be something I wasn't when I was around her. She understood what it was like to grow up differently from everybody else and the challenges we had to face, how we had to fight not to become bitter about life and for people to take us seriously when it came to our dreams. I could tell her about my goals and plans for my future. She was interested in listening to me and would often watch me sign for long minutes, just telling her about things I thought would be annoying to her.

Rebecca never did show if what I shared with her was boring. She wasn't much of a soccer fan, though her uncle Arty was. She liked golf—disc golf to be precise, as did her other uncle,

Josh. They often had competitions to see who was best at the game. Rebecca said she was. I didn't dispute her.

She was just like me. Passionate about what she wanted in life, which wasn't only limited to one thing. She had a checklist of what she wanted to accomplish before she turned thirty and was almost halfway through it. I thought that was awesome. She was hardworking and had a great head on her shoulders.

"I'm lucky I have my uncles. They're the most supportive people ever," Rebecca said as we fed bread to the ducks in the pond in Alton Baker Park.

I was lucky, too, but perhaps not as much as she was. I had my mom, and to me, she was the most supportive person in the world. She was always telling me how proud she was of me. From the moment I was born, she had always fought to protect me. She had risked everything for our family, and I appreciated everything she had done and continued to do for us. I could not have asked for a better mother. I never understood why Margarita never appreciated her.

Rebecca ran out of bread before me, and she rested her head on my shoulder. I didn't notice the weight of her head on my shoulder; neither did I mind the way it hampered the use of my left hand. I was cautious not to disturb her. She was different than Seema, and I liked the way I felt with her. For once in my existence, I felt curiously at ease with life. Not that it was somehow more beautiful. No, it still looked the same, but I thought it was less challenging now. There was a flame burning in me.

CHAPTER 17

Margarita's favorite holiday was Día de Muertos. She told me anyone who has witnessed a proper Day of the Dead would agree that it beats Halloween, hands down. "Día de Muertos has spirits," she would say as Dad's friend, Lupe, drove us to Old Sacramento for the festival in his pickup, "and ghosts."

Margarita always said the word "ghosts" with a smile that sent creepy feelings down my spine. It was her way of preparing Miguel and me for the stories to come later as we made *calaveras de azúcar*, edible sugar skulls. Margarita was a wealth of Mexican folklore, and on other nights, I exchanged chocolates for her tales. It was different on Día de Muertos; she told us the tales willingly, delighting in frightening us. She told us about La Llorona, La Planchada, and the vanishing hitchhiker.

The tale of La Llorona was particularly her favorite, and she had many ways of telling the story of the weeping woman, but always with the same ending.

There are many different variants of the legend, but the one Margarita enjoyed recounting to us most originated in Mexico. "La Llorona is a beautiful woman who wears a white gown and veil," she would begin. "She roams the streets during the evenings and nights, weeping for her children whom she drowned in a river. She was turned away at the gates of the afterlife for her sins and condemned for all eternity to search for their whereabouts, appearing close to rivers and lakes. She roams from the countryside to cities and towns. Men who see her are taken by her beauty, and they follow her until she appears before them, only to lift her veil to reveal her horrid, deathly face, causing them to perish. Some say that when dogs howl in the middle of the night, it is because they have seen La Llorona roaming about. If you hear her crying, you must run away... her wails bring misfortune and death! She kidnaps children she sees wandering at night, mistaking them for her own..." she would say, punctuating the story with a haunting voice and vivid expression.

In every version she told us, she was condemned to roam forever, vainly searching for her children for all eternity. "Forever and ever," Margarita would conclude with a faraway look in her eyes.

I always thought she saw something I didn't. According to me, she was seeing La Llorona, walking the doomed woman's shoes. Her expression scared me more than the tale itself. On our drive back home, she would hug Miguel and sing the song of "La Llorona." I watched her sing it, without fail, and when I went to sleep that night, I played the song back in my head.

When I grew older, Margarita grew more distant, and her tales trickled away to nothing. She went off to college, and there was no one to tell me the story of La Llorona. Miguel was more interested in comic book heroes than he was in the weeping woman. I, too, forgot the stories and the song, only vaguely remembering when I watched Fernando dress up as a ghost for the street Halloween party. I only remembered Día de Muertos was two days away, and I wasn't going.

The day Margarita died wasn't on Día de Muertos, but it rained as it had the last time we'd gone to the festival together, one of the few times Mom had come along. Margarita had made sugar skulls for our *ofrenda* and had marigolds in her hair. Her eyes were bright as she spooked Miguel with the story of La Planchada, ignoring Mom's remonstrations for her to stop. Margarita had only obeyed her once we placed our offerings on the *ofrenda*.

"Abuelo Carlos loved tamales," she whispered to me.

On our way back, she crooned the song again until Miguel fell asleep, and it was the only sound that could be heard in the car until Mom joined in, followed by Lupe. The three of them sang the mournful dirge until Lupe dropped us off at home. As I read Mom's short text, I remembered a part of the song I managed to hear thanks to my hearing aids: *Dicen que no tengo duelo, Llorona, porque no me ven llorar. Dicen que no tengo duelo, Llorona, porque no me ven llorar. Hay muertos que no hacen ruido, Llorona, ¡y es más grande su penar! Hay muertos que no hacen ruido, Llorona, ¡y es más grande su penar!*

The verse was still reverberating in my head when a pillow thumped against it, startling me out of the stupor the news of Margarita's death had put me in. I looked up to see David making faces at me. He seemed to sense something was wrong.

"What's up, Diego? You've been staring at your phone for a long time; it's getting a bit creepy."

I didn't want to put it in words yet in case it was a prank or something, but I knew Mom hated mischievous antics and morbid jokes. I shrugged at him before signing that I had just realized I had made a mistake in Professor Wilson's assignment before handing it in.

David guffawed when he saw the message. "Only you, Diego. Don't worry; he'll probably give you an A regardless. You're his favorite student."

I smiled at him before returning to Mom's text wishing it were all a dream I'd soon wake up from. It wasn't. So, I constructed my response: *I'll be home tomorrow.*

She texted back almost immediately: *Don't, Diego. Stay in school. We'll manage. Just wanted to tell you.*

I'll be home tomorrow, I insisted. *How did Margarita die?* I was hesitant to ask, but I did so anyway. I could already guess what had caused her death, but I wanted to be sure whether or not it had been accidental.

Drug overdose was Mom's reply.

I'll be home tomorrow, I repeated a third time. I was thunderstruck by the news. I wanted to ask Mom how she was holding up, whether Miguel was okay, and if Dad was with them. But I didn't. I only told David that I'd turn in for the night. I pulled the blanket over my head and thought about the last time Margarita had spoken to me. She had sent a text asking me to meet her in a café off campus.

I remembered how thin and frail she had looked. She looked almost emaciated. Her skin was ashy pale, and there were coal-black circles around her eyes, her hair was matted, and she stank. She scratched her arms as she spoke, asking me in a voice devoid of emotions for a few dollars.

"I'll pay you back, Diego. I swear."

I had felt revulsion looking at her, and I flatly denied her requests. As I stood, her voice had risen, and panic and desperation had jumped into her eyes.

"Please, Diego, don't leave. I'll die," she cried, reaching for my hand, but I snatched it away and strode out of the café. That was two weeks ago. I repeatedly asked myself whether she would still be alive had I given her the money she had requested.

"I'll die!" she had cried when she had supplicated me to help her that day. I should have been her brother. I should have helped her. Instead, I had abandoned her, and now she was dead. The guilt ate away at me, and the excuses I had given for leaving her that day no longer mattered. My fury at her for almost getting our parents deported had no relevance at all.

Tears poured from my eyes as I remembered the Margarita of my childhood. Mom had said she would be a lawyer, and she had laughed at that proclamation. She smiled at a lot of things; if only she had laughed at the face of death.

I cried myself to sleep and dreamed of Margarita wandering about for eternity, searching for peace.

"I'm sorry about her death," Fernando said to me, his usually bright face somber. I hadn't seen him in months, and even though I was glad to see him, I would have wanted it to be under different circumstances. I wished to go back to another time when we joked and caused mischief without a care in the world.

"I'm sorry, too," I signed.

There was a moment of uncomfortable silence between us as we sat facing each other in our tiny kitchen.

"If it's not too late, congrats on getting into the U.S. U-20 team," he said.

Fernando had changed a bit. He had a different haircut, having changed it from a bowl to a mullet, and his glasses were gone. Fernando wore contacts now and had gained a bit of weight. Not too much, but he wasn't the skinny boy that had left downtown Sacramento a couple of months ago. I thought he looked like a human-sized pixie.

"Thank you," I gestured with a small smile. "Been hitting the gym?"

"Yeah." He ran a hand through his hair; and that was new too. For a moment, I felt as though I was sitting in front of someone I did not know.

He arrived the day before Margarita's funeral and spent the last night in my former room with Miguel and me after we had put her to rest. For some reason, we hadn't been able to sleep and spent the night playing Uno and then Monopoly in almost utter silence. The silence had been companionable, but the one between us now was different. I expected Fernando to be his usual loquacious self, regaling me with outrageous tales. Instead, he seemed hesitant, as though unsure of how I'd respond to his attempt at joviality.

"I'm fine, Fernando, really," I signed.

"Are you though?" he asked. "I heard your mom tell mine that Margarita had come to your school asking you to loan her a few bucks, but you said no. Now she's dead, and knowing you, you're probably beating yourself over it."

Fernando was right; I was beating myself up over Margarita's death. I couldn't shake the feeling that her demise was my fault, that I could have prevented it if I had been a little more patient and understanding. Margarita had told me that Abuelo Carlos' temper had led to his death. Mine had led to hers.

"Remember when Margarita tried to tell you one of her ghost stories on Halloween? You kept interrupting, and she got angry. You said she should write the story, and she said she would before storming out."

"Yeah," Fernando drawled.

"She wrote it. The cops returned her possessions, and there was a battered little diary among her things. She wrote her stories in it. They needed fine-tuning, and I sent them to an agent. It's the least I could do." A couple of tears dropped on my knuckles, and I angrily wiped them away.

"People will scare themselves silly by reading them," Fernando started, "and one day, they might get adapted into a movie."

I gave a small smile. "Margarita would like that."

There was another stretch of silence, but it wasn't as uncomfortable as the one before it.

"How long will you be in Sacramento?" I asked.

"For the rest of the weekend. I have enough tales to bore you to tears with, and you can tell me about how you got into the U.S. U-20 team."

"It's quite a boring story," I promised him.

"I'll endure it. So, prepare to talk, dude."

Mom entered the kitchen wearing a black dress. She had lost weight in these last couple of days, and like me, she was nursing guilt. Mom had thrown Margarita out when she had come back after the police fiasco. They had a blazing row because of it, and it had our neighbor threatening to call the police. The next time she had heard from Margarita was in a tear-filled message she had left when Mom wouldn't answer her calls. She told Mom she had come to my school, but I wouldn't help her, and if Mom wouldn't help her either, then this would be the last time she and anyone else heard from her. Mom didn't take her threat seriously, just like I hadn't.

She had cried in my arms when I arrived. Dad wasn't at home, and Miguel was at his friend's place. She had insisted he go there, and when he heard I was around, he came back and told me all that had happened between Mom and Margarita.

Dad didn't stay home much again, preferring the company of Luciano and his other friends to the gloomy atmosphere of our abode. He had been drunk at Margarita's funeral. At first, I thought his swaying had been because of his grief. But when I moved closer, I caught the strong scent of alcohol wafting off him. It had repulsed me, and at the same time, I felt sympathy for him. He had indulged her, watched her grow up only for her to be snatched from him. I thought he probably blamed us for her death; that was why he couldn't bear to be in the house with us.

Mom graced Fernando and me with a small smile and mussed my hair to Fernando's amusement. He wouldn't stand for anyone ruffling his hair, and I smirked when Mom did the same to him, and he squirmed in discomfort.

"Are you hungry?" she asked us, her words coming out sluggishly, but we shook our heads, and she drifted out again. I was worried about her. She had trouble sleeping, so she had taken sleeping pills and woke up groggy. Miguel said she sometimes woke at midnight and wandered the house talking to someone who wasn't there. According to him, she was talking to ghosts.

Later that night, in my room, I told Fernando the story of how I had gotten into the U.S. U-20 team. We both sat cross-legged opposite to one another on my bed as he attentively observed me recount the tale of how it had transpired, a broad smile on his face. It was a day I'll never forget. The emotion of finally accomplishing my greatest dream made me feel alive. The tremendous satisfaction of achieving something I had dreamed of since I was a young boy was unlike any other. As I shared the happenings of that memorable day with my best friend, I relived the unforgettable moment again in my mind...

We had just defeated the Oregon State University team on the first game of the season, and that was when the scout saw me. Coach Shaw was beaming. He could hardly contain his excitement when we returned to the locker room and drew me aside with the equally grinning man for a quick chat. I learned I'd been invited to a Youth National Team (YNT) session, and I returned to my dorm in a happy daze.

Coach Shaw followed me to the first session I was invited to and watched me from the bleachers. He gave out encouragement as I played, and I was still whooping when the game ended. I had a feeling they had talked to him when I went to change. His enthusiasm was a little dented, but he still had enough fervor to be buzzing about.

He put his arms around my shoulder when I returned with my duffel bag.

"How would you like to try out to play forward in the U.S. Deaf Men's National Team?" he asked, and I felt a dent in my own rising excitement. To play and compete in the Deaflympics. I can't deny that it was quite an offer, but it wasn't what I wanted.

Simon Ollert played with other players on a regular team. That was what I wanted for myself. It would be excellent playing among people who were deaf just like I was, but I aspired something else. What I sought was a challenge. If I were just going to settle for the USA Deaf Soccer team, I would have just given up on playing for the soccer team in high school the very first time the coach said no. But I had liked the challenge and loved the feeling of overcoming them even more. I thought it was the U.S. U-20 team or nothing. Since I was now seventeen, I could be recruited by scouts for the team.

"I know what you're thinking, Diego," Coach Shaw sighed, letting go of my shoulder to stand in front of me. "But this offer is as good as any other one. U.S. Soccer has never had a deaf player on a regular team before, and I don't think they're going to start now."

"Well, Germany has two," I countered. "Simon Ollert was the second after Stefan Markolf."

Coach Shaw gave me a rueful smile. "This isn't Germany, Diego."

"No, but it's the land of the free. Lionel Messi is—"

"Whoa, kid. Messi isn't deaf."

"But he has a growth hormone deficiency. The point is, they played despite the challenges they faced and are excellent players. I want to be like them. I want to distinguish myself from the rest as they have done."

"It's your call, Diego."

Even though I hadn't gotten what I wanted yet, I was happy I was being considered for the YNT program. The U.S. Soccer YNT Identification Centers events were held every month, and with that out of the way for another month, I focused on regular practice. Often, during breaks, I caught Coach Shaw looking thoughtfully at me. I wondered why I wasn't slacking off in training. If I could say so myself, I felt I was improving with each passing hour.

Even with my devotion to soccer, I wasn't neglectful of my studies. Mom would have a nuclear meltdown if she ever thought I was. David often commented on how he would love to do a brain swap with me. Although he was a bright student, there were still some subjects he struggled with.

"How could someone read this utterly factual textbook?" he would ask me with an air of despair.

I found his reaction to studying exaggerated. Though he told me he'd been a terrible student in high school, he had revamped himself for college. I had seen his test reports. They often had B or A on them—nothing less than a C. He had little difficulty in remembering what he'd previously read. Leslie told me that he was acting like a drama queen, and I was inclined to agree.

Our second game was with Willamette University, and we thoroughly defeated them—in their territory nonetheless. Rebecca came to watch me play this time even though she said she couldn't get the point of putting oneself at risk of breaking bones. Her uncle Arty came too, and he had a slightly glazed look in his bright blue eyes.

"That was good, Diego," he praised. "You are really talented; I have never seen anything like that. The chances you take..." He shook his head. "Well done."

His comment made me happier than a pat on the back. I wished Mom and Miguel were here to watch me play, even if it wasn't at a national level yet. I had texted Mom before the game started, and she wished me luck. She hadn't heard from Margarita, and that was weighing heavily on her heart. I had. Margarita had sent me a few text messages in the past months, but they had been so senseless that I hadn't bothered to reply. I didn't inform Mom about that. She would want her new number so she could call to see if Margarita was okay and if she would be returning to Sacramento. The cops hadn't called them, but ever since that day, they had to take a trip down to the station. Every time I thought of it, I got angry again.

"I think your coach wants to talk to you," Rebecca said, pointing behind me.

I looked back and saw Coach Shaw was indeed waving me over. Standing beside him was a distinguished man who would be more comfortable in an opera house than in a rowdy soccer field.

I asked Rebecca if she would wait, and she must have read it from my eyes or something because she smiled and said that she would remain behind.

"Leslie said she wants to show me something. I think she recorded when that dude took an elbow to the face. It cracked her up," she told me.

I didn't recall when that had occurred. I didn't remember much of what happened on the field; my world often narrowed down to myself and the ball. But even in that haze, I was able to distinguish between opponents and comrades. "Thanks," I signed before leaning to kiss her cheek. I guessed we were sort of dating now; Leslie said we were in the general sense. But dating or not, I loved being with her, and I think it was ditto for her as well. "I'll be right back."

I jogged over to Coach Shaw whose entire body language was a mix of self-satisfaction and excitement.

"Diego, this is Mr. Jenkins from the United States Soccer Federation. Mr. Jenkins, this is our young star, Diego Herrera."

"Hello, Diego, nice to meet you," Mr. Jenkins said in a clipped tone, greeting me with a firm handshake. "I must say I'm very impressed, Shaw. When you told me about him, I admit I was skeptical. It just sounded too good to be true. I'm glad I took the leap of faith and came. You're really outstanding, young man."

I was pretty sure I was the color of a tomato. I forced the wide grin that was threatening to split my face into two away as I strove to appear businesslike.

"Thank you," I signed.

His eyes fell to my moving fingers, and I thought I saw something tighten in his eyes. "Seems Coach Shaw neglected to tell me something."

Coach Shaw made a slight grimace. "Well, I didn't think it was important," he offered lamely, discomfort in his voice.

I felt a hollowness in me as I saw another opportunity passing me by. I was all too accustomed to rejection, and I knew the moment I saw the flash in Mr. Jenkins' eyes when he saw me signing what his answer was going to be.

"But it is," responded Mr. Jenkins. "I am truly sorry. I'm sure there's a place on the Deaflympics for a kid of your talents. Excuse me."

He was turning to leave when Coach Shaw spoke.

"You've seen he is an excellent player. Why won't you give him a chance?"

"He's an exceptional player, and since he's seventeen, he would be perfect for the U-20 Men's National Team if he weren't deaf," Mr. Jenkins said, turning to me with an apologetic look I was very familiar with. "It's not just about talent and potential, as I'm sure you know, Mr. Herrera. It's also about teamwork, and with you unable to hear a thing, it might throw the balance of the team off. It's a risk I'm not willing to take. I'm sorry, Mr. Herrera."

"Balance, unbalance," Coach Shaw scoffed. "You've seen how he played tonight among the other players. Did he throw them off balance? I feel it's unfair that you'd deprive Diego and also the team of a great opportunity."

"Aren't you depriving your school's team of a great opportunity by doing this?"

"We'll manage," Coach Shaw said, shrugging his shoulders. His expression was one of disbelief.

"This is both unfair and discriminatory, Mr. Jenkins. You and I both know that Diego here is probably the finest soccer player you have ever seen in your life. The fact he has a disability does not make him in any way *dis*abled or *in*capable of being a strong asset to U.S. Soccer. He deserves an opportunity just like any other player of his caliber on the field."

Mr. Jenkins was just as astonished by Coach Shaw's passionate argument on my behalf as I was. I was grateful he could speak for me and was willing to fight for what he believed was right. Without a doubt, the world certainly needed more people like him.

"I'm not saying you've convinced me, but I suppose we don't have anything to lose by giving him a shot. Do the first registration and the tryouts after. I suppose that frees me. Good evening, gentlemen."

"And that's how you got in?" Fernando asked.

"That's how I got in," I confirmed, signing.

I remembered the elated emotion I had felt when I'd been accepted. Mr. Jenkins had given me my chance as he promised. Coach Shaw had spoken with him on my behalf to convince him to provide me the opportunity, and I spoke with my skills to convince him of my place in the team.

Coach Shaw had been there with me, and when it was all over, he looked like a proud father.

"They can't tell you no now," he told me. They didn't. How could they?

"I'd buy you a beer if you weren't a minor," Coach Shaw laughed on our way back.

I smiled with him. I didn't need a beer or any other intoxicant; I was already drunk on happiness.

CHAPTER 18

"How did your parents react to you joining the National Team?" David asked as he was trashing me in checkers. It was just the two of us alone in the dorm. Leslie was away in New York for the week, and we weren't expecting her until Friday. Rebecca was studying for a test. We were supposed to as well, but laziness set in, and we found ourselves pushing our books aside to break in the checkerboard David had bought.

"They were... cool with it," I paused in my game to sign.

That was the understatement of the century. My parents hadn't blown up, but they didn't react in the way I'd expected them to. I told them the night before I returned to Oregon. Postponing breaking the news to them would have meant having to do it over text or waiting until Easter. Dad hadn't cared at all about my story. He wasn't even around the night before I left; it was only Mom and Miguel.

"That's so cool," Miguel praised, his face awestruck. "So, does this mean we're going to be seeing you on TV now?"

"I don't know about that," I answered honestly. "But probably."

"Awesome!"

"I don't understand," Mom finally decided to say. "What about your education?" she asked, making an effort for me. She had just taken her antidepressants and was feeling drowsy.

"It's going to be fine," I assured her.

The drugs made her slow, so it took a while before she understood the words I signed.

"Well, if you're certain about that," she said, her eyes drooping shut.

The emotion I felt was bittersweet. I was happy Mom had enough trust in me but sad that she was still beating herself up over Margarita's death. With Dad away with his drinking buddies most of the time and Mom being like this, I wondered how Miguel was coping. It must be tough on him. He had just lost a sister, and instead of rallying around him, Mom was riddled with guilt, Dad was distant, and I, his older brother, was away in college.

I looked into his brown eyes; they were full of love and support. I felt blessed. Mom was still sleeping when I returned to Oregon. Miguel saw me off to the car.

"Wait till I tell my classmates about this," he said to me, stepping back for me to start the car.

I watched him grow smaller and smaller in the rearview mirror until he disappeared from view. My heart ached for him.

I didn't tell anyone what had happened and that I had to go home. I'd only told Rebecca and Gibson since I had to take a week off from work. He had been sufficiently sympathetic. I told Rebecca over a text message, and she wanted to come with me, but I dissuaded her. I was sure she would have informed David and Leslie why I had to rush off home. Even if she didn't want to, Leslie had a way of extracting information from an unwilling informant.

Leslie succeeded. David was in our dorm with Leslie when I let myself in. Their jovial expression dropped, and I saw sympathy before they pulled it back up.

"Hey, Diego. How was the trip home?" David asked, aware of the elephant in the room, but Leslie was as subtle as a raging rhinoceros. She wasn't one for walking on eggshells.

"Why didn't you tell us?" she asked, her face soft with sympathy.

"I didn't want it to be true," I admitted, signing after tossing my bag onto my bed. "But it is."

"How did she die?" Leslie asked.

"Overdose," I signed.

"Oh."

There was an awkward silence in the room.

"So, what has happened since I was gone?" I asked.

"I wrote a new poem," David told me. "It's titled 'Begone, Leslie!'"

"Sounds cool," I signed.

"Don't indulge him," Leslie scolded me.

I laughed. Leslie and David really had a good sense of humor, and I enjoyed every moment of their company. I had always dreamed of having friends; it was apparent that I had found them.

They didn't try to walk on eggshells around me, and I was grateful for that. It would have made it awkward. Mom sent a text message to me later that night. It was short, but she was only reaffirming that she was proud of me. It made me glow with happiness.

Apart from the first day, David and Leslie didn't bother questioning me about Margarita. They let me mourn her in peace, acting with me as they usually did. I appreciated it.

It had been five days since I'd returned from Sacramento when we decided to play checkers.

"How are your new teammates? Are they nice?"

I had been introduced to my new teammates. I had never found a more supportive team to belong to. In high school, my teammates had been wary at best before they accepted me. In college, they were skeptical of me at first, although we weren't friends yet, except for Brayden. They were amicable. The U-20 team welcomed me with open arms.

There was an ovation when I was introduced, and they took turns in patting me on the back, welcoming me into their fold. There were some adjustments made to the team's routine because of me, but they didn't seem to mind that their set schedule was rearranged. For one, they started taking a sign language class so they would be able to understand me when I communicated.

They showed me what they could do and ended up making up obscure symbols with ludicrous meanings. I felt like I'd known them for years with the way they treated me. I couldn't remember being nervous about meeting them, as they made me feel completely relaxed and welcome. They weren't overly fascinated about my life but moderately curious about my story. Each of them was as talented as I was or compensated for their weaknesses with hard work, but they were in awe of my talent. And sometimes, when I tried out a move, I was always mobbed by questions as to how I did it and requests to repeat it.

Due to a team member being unable to play because of an injury, I was added to the final roster for the twenty playing in the 2018 CONCACAF Under-20 Championship starting in November. It was the qualification tournament for the FIFA U-20 World Cup next year, and I was ecstatic. I couldn't believe my luck. The scouts of the big clubs came to watch the games for players they could sign up, and with luck, I could become affiliated with Major League Soccer. My squad number was number 10.

The same as Lionel Messi's, and that fact made me glow.

"I'll come to watch you whenever I can," Rebecca promised me, echoing the promise David and Leslie had made to me.

"I would love that," I signed. The idea of having my friends cheering me on was something that filled me with emotion.

I took a leave of absence from school, since I'd be busy with the tournament, and got ready for the new chapter in my life. I had never been so excited about anything in my life, and I couldn't wait for it to begin.

The United States was hosting the 2018 CONCACAF tournament, so there was no need to travel. I felt a little let down, as I would have loved to travel outside the country. Costa Rica had hosted last year's tournament, and I had followed it closely on TV. The tournament had thirty-four teams participating. Based on the CONCACAF men's U 20 ranking, the top six ranked teams were seeded into position one of each group, while the remaining twenty-eight teams were distributed in five pots.

It was hosted in Bradenton, Florida, between the first to twenty-first of November. The United States had been the champions of last year's tournament, with Honduras coming as runners-up, but Mexico had more wins, and that gave me a sense of pride. Last year, they added a second group stage to the competition format, with the winners and runners-up of this stage qualifying for the U-20 World Cup, and the winners would secure a place in the final. Playing in the World Cup was the epitome of this checklist. Everyone naturally wants to win, and we were no exception.

Fernando came for the first round of the tournament, the first time the U.S. team was going to play. He came with a girl I thought was his girlfriend, but I wasn't entirely sure.

Thirty minutes before the game started, I felt sick, and James, the goalkeeper, gave me a paper bag to use to ease my breathing.

"Do you need to throw up?" he asked me.

I shook my head, surprised at how sweaty I was. "I don't think so," I gestured.

"Well, if you need to, be sure to do it before the head coach starts his pep talk."

I was good. I wasn't feeling nauseous, just a bit dizzy, and wondering if I'd be able to pull this off.

The head coach, Adam Rennicks, was exactly like Coach Miller. When I first saw him, I wondered if he'd gone to the same school as Coach Miller, as if he was channeling him. He was gruff, curt, and expected nothing but the best. Heaven have mercy if you fell short. I had heard horror stories of how he had reduced a rookie to tears. Adam hadn't provoked anyone to the point of crying in my presence, but I could see the head coach was tough. Adam was even tougher on me than Coach Miller had been, but he certainly didn't drive me to tears.

Adam made me understand that I had many expectations to live up to. I was the first deaf person on the United States Men's National Soccer Team, and there would be a lot of eyes on me. They would be watching, weighing to see how I performed. Waiting to see whether a great performance on my part paid off the risk everyone on the team had taken to include me, and become a beacon of hope and inspiration for others like me. Or if I failed bitterly, maybe ending my career before it even began, and being shunned by others.

He continually reminded me that I only had this one shot. Just one single opportunity, and if I squandered it, I wouldn't get any other chance. I let that be my mantra. I had a lot riding on this; it was the one-way ticket to fulfilling my dreams, and I couldn't fail. So, I trained harder, knowing that my success could mean an open door for others like me that wanted the opportunity but were too scared to try. I was going to open the door for them. Every time I felt like calling it quits, I would imagine Mom's face beaming with pride. I would remember the feeling I felt the first time I played before a crowd. Those memories kept me going.

Adam was impressed that I was taking his words to heart. He developed strategies for the game with the team's captain and the assistant coaches. They covered all the what-ifs and maybes, and we practiced until we could move like that in our sleep. The United States was the defending champion, and we were determined to keep that title.

Our first match was with Puerto Rico, and as we marched out, I started feeling nausea. *Oh no,* I thought, shutting my eyes against the unease. I tried calming myself by thinking it was just nerves. I wasn't going to throw up and embarrass myself in front of the people who had come to cheer for the U.S.A. and the journalists and reporters. I imagined Mom's face if she were to see me vomit on national TV. Miguel wouldn't think that was cool or awesome. Those mental images did not make me feel any better.

There was a fuzzy thing before my eyes when everyone rose to sing the national anthem. My heart was pounding against my sweaty palm. *I can't do this,* I thought, and I felt like crying. My breathing had gotten heavier. I scanned the crowd for a familiar face but couldn't find any. The world was blurring until it was just me, and I was shivering with fear. *I can't do this,* I thought. *I can't quit now.* One part of me was trying to encourage the rest of me to get it together. *There's no time. You're going to have to do it, Die-go.* For some reason, I thought it was Margarita talking to me. I could see her in front of me as clear as day; she had her storyteller's face on.

"There was once a boy named Diego who thought he couldn't do it," she was saying. "Everyone told him he couldn't. But he could, and when the day came for him to prove that he could, he pulled his head out from the clouds and into the game."

"Get your head in the game, Diego!" It was Adam now, and he was scowling at me.

"You can do it, Diego, my Dieguito." Adam morphed into Mom, and she was cheering me on. "You can do it, Diego. Go, Diego!" It felt like everyone in my life was standing before me in a row and cheering for me.

Till my dying day, I will forever cringe whenever I remember how the first few minutes of the game went. I made many dribbling errors. I was only glad and relieved my few minutes of mistakes didn't cost us much. I could only imagine the frustrated yelling from everyone at my stupid antics. In those few minutes, I felt like an old computer that was rebooting, and when I finally did, I was back to my old self—or at least somewhat.

By the time the game was over, no one had remembered my hiccup except Adam and those that might have recorded it. We beat Puerto Rico seven to one. While others celebrated, Adam glared at me.

"What happened out there, Diego?" he asked me, his gaze alight with bewilderment. I was half afraid that this was it and that he would kick me out of the team.

I offered no explanation. Adam had no tolerance for excuses. So, I waited for the ax to fall. It didn't. I got off with a warning, and after he yelled at the others that it wasn't yet time to celebrate, he strode off.

Later, while everyone else had passed out from exhaustion, I was awake and scribbling about the day's events in my diary.

The next game was on the third of November between U.S. Virgin Islands and us. I didn't have my panic attack before the match began, and my playing was more like myself. Our opponents suffered a crushing defeat at our hands. Thirteen to nil.

With each match, I felt like I was improving, evolving into a more mature version of myself—a self-assured me with greater self-confidence who was ready to take on the world. I played like I had never before, giving my all with each game. And with each subsequent game, I had more to offer. We defeated the teams from Trinidad and Tobago, Saint Vincent and the Grenadines, and Suriname.

The finals were on the twenty-first of November at 7:00 p.m., and it was against Mexico. It was a close battle, but we still emerged victors for the second time running. This time, Adam allowed us to run wild with our celebration. I couldn't be happier.

As we hoisted the cup, I felt like my heart was soaring. I had my own personal award, as well—the CONCACAF Golden Ball for best player. My teammates lifted me into the air as they had done the cup, all their hands reaching to touch. I cried tears of joy.

CHAPTER 19

"Oh-oh!" Leslie exclaimed. "Fan alert. Two blonds headed to the table."

I had slumped forward in my chair, my hand resting on the page I was supposed to be reading but was too tired to.

"Come on, Diego. Put on your best face."

I didn't take the trouble to remind her that I had a girlfriend, and Rebecca was her friend. I wasn't sure I could look attractive. I had dark circles under my eyes, and I was positive my pupils were dilated from the countless cups of coffee I had drunk to keep myself awake. There was also the stubble. I hadn't shaved in two days, and the skin on my face was unbearably itchy.

This was my life now. After the CONCACAF tournament, it was as though people had become aware of me. Adam was right. I could either make it or break it, and I made it. We held a press conference the morning after we won the tournament, followed by personal interviews with each of the team members.

I felt nervous during the interview—the kind of nervousness that settled like a brick in my stomach and made my fingers stiff. I got through it, and after a few more shots with a fixed smile, I was free to seek out Fernando. He had only made it to three matches: the one at the beginning, the one after that, and the finals. He was one of the people that recorded my antics, and he gleefully showed them to me. In retrospect, I admit it was funny, but then, it had been plainly embarrassing.

"You're doing it, Diego. Just like you said you would."

Miguel borrowed his friend's laptop and skyped me. He was brimming with so much excitement I thought he would burst. When he dragged Mom into joining the conversation, I could see she was getting better, and I was glad about that.

"We are proud of you, Diego. So proud." Her eyes went misty with tears, and she excused herself, so she could wipe them.

Rebecca, David, and Leslie had also come to watch the finals, but they hadn't informed me.

"We didn't want to throw you off your game, bro," David explained when I asked why. "Who knows, you might be overcome with the urge to impress your girl that you'd put on a repeat of what happened in the beginning."

I scowled at him.

"You were impressive, Diego, both as the meme king and soccer player. I won't lie… but I still don't like soccer."

"You and everyone I'm friends with," I told him.

The photos had graced the cover of December's edition of *Soccer America,* and inside was the in-depth interviews we had with the journalists. Before I knew it, everything exploded. It started with random people gawking at me and sniggering, and that was when I knew that they had seen the funny video. Journalists soon started showing up where I worked, then there were requests for interviews, and sometimes people stalked in bushes and hedges to take pictures of me.

"You don't know what you've done, do you?" Rebecca asked as we walked to the Ya-Po-Ah Terrace, the tallest building in downtown Oregon.

"I don't," I signed, but that wasn't entirely true. I had some idea as to what I had done.

"Diego, you're the first deaf person to be a member of the U.S. U-20 Men's National Soccer Team. Not only are you a member, but you also participated with the U.S. team in the CONCACAF Championship and were victorious!"

"Team effort," I reminded her.

She waved it away. "Then you were awarded the CONCACAF Golden Ball. And we know that's only for the best players. Naturally, people would be curious about you and want to use your image."

"Still weird, my first trip to limelight was a weird video of me," I signed.

"There's no such thing as bad publicity," Rebecca said sagely with a straight face. "Everybody wants to know you now. Diego, the rising star," she quoted from the magazine. "At least everyone who watches sports and makes a big deal out of soccer. Not regular people like David and me that can't understand a single thing about it."

"Don't take the joy out of it," I signed.

"I wouldn't do that to you, Diego. Just promise me one thing. I want you to speak at this fundraiser I'm planning. You know, before others start asking you to. I'm the first to ask."

"So, you'd like me to give a speech?"

"Of course." Rebecca was unabashed. "Do you wonder if any paparazzi are lurking in the bushes over there? What would be the headline in their tabloid, I wonder? *Rising star Diego Herrera enjoys a stroll in the park with girlfriend*—or something like that."

"Shut up," I signed to her. She laughed.

Rebecca was correct in her prediction. The world was curious about me, and they did what people who are interested do best. They dug into my life. David and Leslie found the new invasion of my privacy amusing, finding new names to tease me with. Little Starlet, Rising Star, and Jackie Soccer because I was the Jackie Chan of soccer. Their favorite moniker was Rising Star. It was funny to them.

It wasn't only me who was hounded. David had been accosted at the gas station where he stopped to fill up his car. It wasn't until Leslie threatened to run them over with the car, starting up the vehicle to prove her point, that they dispersed. Fernando texted me that a reporter had discovered our friendship and was asking questions about me. It was a bit funny knowing the media had gone that far. I was only glad they hadn't found my family yet. But it worried me that if they were doing so much digging, they would find out my parents were illegal immigrants. It suddenly wasn't that funny anymore.

It wasn't only reporters; it was organizations as well. I was soon getting invitations to speak at fundraisers and conferences; people began asking for permission to use my name to boost their brand. The sudden attention was almost unnerving.

I was true to my word. Rebecca's fundraiser was the first I would speak at, and that was later tonight. I suddenly sprang up. I hadn't completed writing my speech. David was helping me with it earlier until he became lazy and told me to follow my heart before going to sleep. Leslie was too busy to help me, and now immersed in the study of the mind, I had forgotten.

"Hi, Diego," one of the blond girls said with a friendly smile. The other stayed behind with a nervous smile on her face.

I waved at her instead of signing.

"I'm Diana, and this is Ariel. I apologize if we're intruding."

I shrugged to show it wasn't a problem.

"We saw the CONCACAF finals, and I want to tell you, the

way you scored that last goal was simply amazing."

I smiled.

"Do you mind signing this?" She dug into her messenger bag and brought out a copy of *Soccer America*, then handed it to me.

I scribbled my signature on it and handed it back.

"Thank you." She turned back to Ariel, and there was a silent communication between the two. Diana moved out of view, and Ariel gave me her shy and hesitant smile.

"Hi," she signed.

"Hi. You know sign language?" I asked, gesturing.

"Yeah. I was born deaf. I just wanted to say it was a courageous thing you did, trying out for the U.S. U-20 team even though there has never been a deaf player on the team. I know many kids who are inspired by what you did. Thank you."

Her words almost moved me to tears. "Thank you, Ariel."

She beamed. They both left.

"That was interesting," Leslie commented. "Do you think Diana would date David? She is kinda cute, but David is so weird. What do you think?"

"I refuse to be drawn into your matchmaking scheme," I signed.

"But I'm so good at it. Take you and Rebecca, for example."

"Rebecca and I met at the café I work at," I informed her.

"A café I got you a job at. So, you see, all part of my scheme. But seriously, I think Diana would totally go for David."

"No comment," I signed.

"Speaking of couples, do you plan on going to Rebecca's fundraiser looking like something the cat dragged in?"

For some reason, the mention of the word cat made me think of Gordo, and I smiled.

"What are you smiling at; how Rebecca would skin you if

you showed up looking like that?"

"I still have about three hours before I have to be there. If I leave now, I'll be able to take a shower and shave."

"And finish writing your speech?"

"That also." I started packing up my books and stuffing them into my backpack. "You'll also be there, right?" I signed before zipping up my bag.

"Sure, and with a camcorder. I want to be the first to catch it on camera if you give us something else to brighten our moods with."

"Funny," I signed.

Rebecca had organized a previous fundraiser on raising awareness for rheumatoid arthritis, and I had been saddened to miss it. I was glad this one was before I'd have to go home for Christmas. Rebecca lived in Eugene, and she was talking about one last fundraiser before the new year. This one was to raise funds for deaf children, and it was happening in the WOW Hall. This time, she was partnering with *Hearing Our Way*, a magazine that focused on children who have hearing impairments. She thought I would be the perfect candidate to give a speech. I was touched by her trust in me.

I felt things were moving faster than I'd ever imagined. The champion of CONCACAF automatically gets qualified for the U-20 World Cup. It would be starting on May 23 and ending by June 15. I was already pumped even though the roster wasn't out yet.

It took me an hour to get ready, and I spent another hour putting the finishing touches on my speech. Rebecca wanted me to be there before the event started, and I made it to the WOW Hall with thirty minutes to spare.

"Hey, Diego. Let me introduce you to Ms. Bloomer. She's

the brains behind *Hearing Our Way.*"

Ms. Bloomer was a tall, thin lady with the face of the secretary in those old movies. She was also deaf, so we communicated with sign language.

"Well, Mr. Herrera. I would be glad if after this you grant us an interview. It would mean the world to our readers."

I nodded my assent.

Leslie and David arrived a few minutes before the program started. The she-devil brought a camera like she had threatened, raising her eyebrows at me when she saw I was glowering at her.

To Leslie's great disappointment, and my relief, the program went off without a hitch. I did not give any new meme material, but I thought I touched people's hearts.

I was a bit nervous when it was time to give my speech. Since there weren't just deaf or hard of hearing people in the audience, Rebecca interpreted my words. David had advised my statement to be about myself, my trials, and my triumphs. As I stood before the upturned faces looking eagerly at me, I tucked the written speech back in my pocket and followed David's advice.

"Hi," I signed. "My name is Juan Diego Herrera, and I was born deaf..."

CHAPTER 20

"Hey, you're Diego, right?"

I set the cup of coffee before me, wondering why he was asking. He was dressed to the teeth like a prosperous business-man, and he proceeded to pull a glossy magazine from his leather attaché case. I recognized it as this month's edition of *Sports Illustrated*, and I was gracing the cover. I felt my ears turn red with embarrassment by his enthusiasm.

"Could you sign this?" he requested, holding out a fountain pen to me. "It's for my son. His name is Adrian, and he's a big fan of yours."

I nodded, taking the pen from him.

"Thank you."

His eagerness made me feel uncomfortable. I signed my name on the front page along with a little inscription that said *Follow your dreams, Adrian.*

"Thank you," he smiled, taking his pen back. "I really appreciate it."

"Another one of your fans?" Mario asked. "He doesn't seem like the usual kind that waits at the curb for you to clock in."

"It's for his son," I wrote on my pad, then showed it to him.

"Well, don't let Gibson get a whiff of him or he'll go crazy. He had a trying time shoveling one of your raving fans off the café's doorstep after your shift ended yesterday, and he's in a grumpy mood today."

I knew they were a menace. The paparazzi weren't allowed on the school grounds, but somehow my face managed to get on blogs and tabloids. They stalked me on my way to work and also when David, Leslie, and I went out on the town.

"I just hope I don't get fired because of them," I wrote.

"Nah. You bring in the customers. Gibson would prefer to part with his left foot."

The man in fancy attire was still there when my shift ended. He hadn't drunk his coffee yet and appeared nervous.

"Maybe he wants to talk to you," Mario guessed.

He did.

"Hi again," he said when I went to him. He still had a nervous energy about him. "I'm Christopher Wilkins. Could I ask a favor of you? It's something simple. You see, my son, he is just like you. By that, I mean he's deaf and uses sign language to communicate, and he also loves soccer. But lately, he has been depressed, and we can't get him to say what's wrong. Since he looks up to you, I thought you could talk to him. That is if you have the time and if you wouldn't mind."

<hr />

"So, how old is this boy?" David asked me.

"He is eleven," I signed. "And a huge fan of soccer."

"And you apparently," Leslie put in. She was shuffling a deck of cards and trying to perform her magic tricks on Rebecca, who was looking skeptical about the whole thing. "Pick a card," she ordered.

I squirmed a bit when Leslie said: *and you apparently.* I wasn't used to the thought of people actually looking up to me. I knew I had come farther than most, academically and in soccer. If Fernando were here, he would say something along the lines of everything being a result of luck and bullheadedness. He had sent me a laughing emoji when I told him about the interview I gave in *Hearing Our Way* and *The Endeavor*. Both were magazines for the deaf and hard of hearing. He read both interviews and later sent me a thumbs-up emoticon. He would probably break one or two ribs in laughter when I told him about this.

To be honest, I was a bit nervous about the whole idea of trying to talk to a young boy and give him life advice. Leslie told me to just be myself; there was no more significant advice than that. But at that moment, I thought it wasn't at all helpful. She didn't mind in the least when I said her suggestion was silly.

"Both of you have a lot of things in common. You share a vast expanse of common ground. The only thing different is he's eleven and rich."

"And he goes to a private school," David added.

"Point is, you are a lovable person, and the kid idolizes you. It might start out a little awkward and stilted, but you'll end up doing what needs to be done. Now, it's not what you are going to do that matters, it's what you're going to wear." She finished reshuffling the cards, yanking out a glossy one and presenting it to Rebecca with a flourish. "Is this your card?"

Rebecca shook her head.

I ended up wearing khakis again for my Saturday visit to the Wilkins' residence. David wanted me to wear clothes I could roll around in, but I wasn't sure what he meant. I was so preoccupied with how the meeting was going to go, and I couldn't care less if I showed up at their doorstep wearing burlap. None of the advice Leslie and Rebecca had given me to stop fretting helped. David kindly offered to drop me off at the Wilkins' so I wouldn't "crash my car while fretting."

They lived in a large French-style villa; the place had a home-ly appeal to it that made me feel a little better.

David put his head out of the car window. "Text me about thirty minutes before you're done. See you later, dude, and good luck."

I watched him drive off before I walked up the stairway and pushed my finger against the doorbell. A portly elderly woman wearing a floral gown and a plaid kerchief over her snow-white hair answered the door. Her eyes did a quick sweep over me, lingering for a second on one of my hearing aids before looking into my eyes.

"You must be Diego Herrera," she said at last and stepped aside for me to enter. "Come in," she invited.

"Thank you," I signed. Mr. Wilkins had informed me that everyone in their household understood sign language. They thought it was a way to help Adrian feel more included. When he was home from school, they all used sign language, only talking when necessary.

"Adrian is waiting for you upstairs; I'll take you to him. Follow me."

We climbed a spiral staircase to the second level and down a carpeted hallway before pausing in front of a door. She pressed at a buzzer until a light began to flash, then pushed the door open and gestured me in.

I felt like I'd stepped into a soccer Narnia. The room was painted in black and white and excessively plastered with posters of clubs, soccer teams, and soccer players, whose faces—including my own—stared down at me. Soccer paraphernalia hung from the ceiling, the walls, adorned the shelves, and littered the floor. I kicked a soccer ball as I walked in, and then kneeled to pick it up. There was a signature on it—Lionel Messi. I felt lighthearted as I saw it, feeling the fanboy in me come out. Apart from Simon Ollert, Lionel Messi was my second favorite player. His accomplishments astonished me, and that was the level I was aiming for or higher. Apart from his prodigious soccer skills, I felt I could relate to him. Although he had a growth hormone deficiency, that hadn't stopped him from reaching for the stars. Likewise, I wasn't going to let my disability stop me from achieving my dreams. I felt slightly jealous that Adrian had met Lionel Messi and gotten his signature.

Adrian was standing by a foosball table, pretending I wasn't in the room with him. I couldn't see his face because he was ducking down, but I could see his ears were red. He was nervous, just like me, and I started feeling a lot better.

I dropped the soccer ball on the floor and approached the foosball table. We briefly stood on opposite ends before he looked up and then swiftly looked away without meeting my eyes.

"Do you play?" he suddenly signed, his finger movements a bit stilted.

"No," I gestured back. It had been the one game I wanted to try, yet kept forgetting. "But it should be easy, shouldn't it?"

Adrian nodded. "Do you want to play?"

"Why not?" I signed. "I'll be the blue team."

I was brutally defeated in the first game. Adrian, amazed that his idol could be terrible at something, started withdrawing from his shell and began to enjoy himself. I started getting the hang of the game in the second round and put up enough fight so that my sound defeat wasn't so embarrassing this time around. We played ten times, and I only won once. Adrian grinned after the game and bounded excitedly around the room in a celebratory dance.

"You lost really bad," he signed, grinning widely.

"I won once, I put up a good fight," I protested, signing.

"Lost!" he repeated. "I'd probably beat you in soccer as well," he signed with an impish grin.

"Bring it on," I gestured.

We played soccer in his backyard. Adrian's parents had allocated a space in the seemingly endless green land for soccer playing with goalposts and stuff. I won most of it, letting him win a few. He caught on with what I was doing and protested, telling me not to go easy on him. He still won a few after that, though I hadn't played at the fullest of my capacity.

Exhausted, we flopped down on the grass, side by side, and stared up at the azure sky, trying to get our breath back. I was no longer feeling nervous. About five minutes later, Adrian sat up, and I followed suit. There was a grim expression on his face as he stared into the distance, pulling at the grass. I waited for him to be ready to communicate.

"I want to be a soccer player," he signed, confessing to me.

"That's great," I told him, followed by a double thumbs-up.

"But I can't," he admitted gravely.

I was puzzled by his remark. "Why not?"

He drew his knees up and placed his chin on them before signing, "I'm weak."

I didn't stop him as he continued signing, telling me his story. His parents weren't often at home, so he was mostly his only company. He used to go to a regular private school but was bullied so bad, his parents had to withdraw him. They tried homeschooling for a while, but that didn't work. His tutor wasn't as patient with him as he should be, and he also endured bullying from him until his parents realized what was going on and fired him. He was stubborn and refused to cooperate with his other tutors, so they had no choice but to enroll him in a special-needs school.

"They are supportive," he admitted to me. "But I have a hard time making friends. In my old school, some used to pretend to be my friend, so they could hurt me, and now I can't trust anyone. I think the only thing I can trust is soccer, but I don't think I'm good enough to play. Mr. Walters, my first tutor, said I would never be good enough to play."

Leslie had told me to be myself. I had a common ground with Adrian. So, in return, I told him about my life. I told him about the little bungalow where I grew up in downtown Sacramento and the tiny bedroom I had shared with Margarita and Miguel. I told him how nervous I had been to start school, how the principal had advised a special-needs school, but my mom had stuck with her decision to have me in a regular school. I told him how I had been treated differently and bullied like he had been.

Soccer was my only solace, but I wouldn't be let on the team because of my disability. I told him of how I'd kept trying and trying even when the coach asked me to give up, telling me that I couldn't be on the team. I told him how I'd finally got in during my last year in school and how my teammates accepted me. I told him about the soccer team in college and how scared I had been about transitioning. I told him about being advised to try out for the U.S. deaf soccer team, which I refused. Then I had gotten noticed during a game and had to try harder than anyone else on the U-20 Men's National Team. I told him about Fernando, David, Leslie, Rebecca, and my coworkers at the café where I worked part-time.

"I made my first friend when I was about your age, I think

slightly older," I gestured. Even though my fingers were aching, I continued. "Never let them say you can't do it, Adrian, because you know deep down inside that you can, no matter what odds you face. You only need one person to have faith in you, and that is yourself."

About half an hour after sending him a text message, David came to pick me up.

"How did it go?" David asked as he drove me back.

"It was nice," I signed after giving thought to how it had gone. "Adrian is a bright kid. He's a vegetarian like you. You'd like him."

David smiled amusedly. "Well, I'm glad I'd like him... because vegetarians rock!"

"Well, his only other interests are soccer and collecting stamps. He'll be okay," I added.

CHAPTER 21

I stared at the picture Adrian had just texted me; it was a picture of him with the new soccer ball his dad bought him as an early Christmas gift. I wished someone would think of buying me a new soccer ball. Rebecca had given me a scarf before I went home for Christmas. It was bright yellow and very thick. I didn't like it, but Rebecca had made it herself, so I had to wear it. I was glad Sacramento was hot so I wouldn't have to use it. The last thing I needed was Fernando laughing at me when we were supposed to be having a tearful reunion. A few of my fans sent gifts through the mail before I left. Their thoughtfulness was really heartwarming.

Rebecca, David, Leslie, and I went Christmas shopping to purchase gifts to give to our friends and loved ones. As a member of the U-20 MNT, I was paid a certain amount. Combined with my savings, I had more than enough to splurge on gifts.

"Are you sure you're not buying for an army?" David said lightheartedly, eyeing the items over.

"Five," I corrected, holding my hand up and splaying my fingers.

"I'm not helping you wrap those," he told me.

I shrugged.

I bought a state-of-the-art camera for Fernando. Miguel's

gift was his very own laptop. I couldn't think of a present good enough for Mom. So, I decided to buy her a necklace and a host of other things. Margarita's book had already been published and was a success, so I bought Mom a copy. The publisher had previously sent one to me. I cried when I read it, but it helped me cope with Margarita's death. I was sure it would do the same for Mom. I bought Dad a fully stocked toolbox like the one he'd always wanted.

Rebecca and I had already exchanged gifts. She had given me the scarf, and I had given her a carving. I'd found it at an art exhibit that her uncle, Arty, had invited me to. It was a simple carving, but it reminded me of Rebecca so much I had to buy it. It was a carving of a rosebud opening up, and emerging from the center was a woman bearing another rosebud. Rebecca peppered my face with kisses when I gave it to her. It was small enough to be worn as a pendant, and the next day, before leaving for Sacramento, I'd seen her wearing it on a chain.

David didn't celebrate Christmas and told me not to get him a Christmas gift, but he got me a new pair of cleats and a yoga mat to remind me not to forsake yoga when I went home. Leslie bought me a pair of Nike boots, and I gave her a charm bracelet.

Despite saying he wouldn't, David helped me gift-wrap most of the items, though he grumbled from beginning to end. We then binge-watched Christmas movies till past midnight. He gave me some chocolate bars and several bottles of cold-brewed coffee so I wouldn't fall asleep while I drove back home to Sacramento.

"What are you doing on Christmas?" I signed at him before we started lugging my bags to my Cavalier.

"I'm spending it with my grandfather. If it gets too tiring, you'll see me on your doorstep."

When I got home, Mom was already at the door. For a moment, she stood in the doorway, her eyes wide with surprise.

"Papa?" she asked, her eyes rapidly filling with tears.

"Mom?"

The realization came to her eyes, as well as a red flush to her face. She pulled me into an embrace, and we tried to forget she had just called me her dad. Later, while everyone was asleep, I wrote in my journal. Still curious as to what Mom had seen, I went to the bathroom. Standing in front of the mirror, I looked at my reflection and was almost startled at the change. It wasn't as if I hadn't seen myself in a mirror before. Most of the time, I gave my reflection a cursory glance on my way to class. I never really looked at myself as I did now. All I could think of was that the old Diego was gone.

I had grown several inches over the last few months, and the training had given me lean but defined muscles. I looked like a man, no longer a boy, and my stubble didn't help matters. I could only marvel as to how much I'd grown, and it wasn't only physically. It was also mentally and emotionally. As I walked to Fernando's house, I felt a newfound sense of confidence in the way I held myself and in the way I walked.

Fernando commented on it also.

"You've changed, Diego. But too bad your chess skills haven't," he teased as he wiped me off the board.

I saw Seema when I accompanied Mom to her work. I didn't feel the anger and spitefulness at her anymore and waved. She seemed relieved when I did, and we had a small chat before she had to leave.

Mom bought a turkey to prepare for Christmas dinner. She wanted us to have a traditional Christmas this year, with a Christmas tree, decorations, and stockings hung up, even though our family had been knocked down a few pegs. Dad had moved out, and Mom didn't know where he'd gone. He just up and left in the middle of the night. Mom didn't bother searching for him.

"Your father is a grown man, Diego. He has a mind and heart of his own. If he's going to come back, well, the door is open for him. He hasn't been kidnapped. His clothes are missing, and Lupe called me. Alejandro stayed a few days in his house before leaving."

So, it would be Mom, Miguel, and me celebrating Christmas as a family. It didn't sound so bad. My plan to sleep in on Christmas was interrupted when I was awoken by grasping hands. Fernando was somehow in my room and yanking on my arms.

We sat on the floor in the living room, next to the tree and unwrapped presents. I got a box of chocolates from Miguel and another pair of cleats from Mom. I tried not to show that I didn't really like them. I felt I had more than enough pairs to last me a lifetime.

Miguel was beyond ecstatic over his new laptop and bowled me over with his hug before he regained control of himself and promptly turned on the device. Mom gave me a teary smile when she opened her gifts, and then she hugged me tightly. Fernando punched me lightly in the arm before handing me my present. They were an awesome looking pair of hearing aids in a gleaming blue color.

"Not that anything's wrong with the pair you have. I just thought, you know, with a new chapter of your life and all, it deserves a new pair of hearing aids to help you through."

As I took out my old pair, I remembered how Margarita had once said my hearing aids were ugly. Fernando set up his camera as I put them on and took a picture of me. He had to leave because he had promised to help his mom with cooking.

David did show up on my doorstep on Christmas Day. I remembered how shocked I was to see him standing there and grinning as if there was nothing out of the ordinary going on.

"My granddad is leaving for Taipei today. I wasn't in the mood for intercontinental travel, so here I am."

"Why not go to Leslie's?" I signed to him.

"Didn't she tell you? She went with her parents to London to see her grandparents. And Rebecca's gone to spend Christmas with her dad. I'm not going to intrude on father-daughter bonding time."

"How did you find my place? I don't remember giving you the address."

"You gave it to Rebecca. Rebecca forwarded it to me. I brought presents."

I smiled and held the door open for him to come in.

Mom didn't know how to react with David. Knowing her well, I was aware she could see he was born with a silver spoon in his mouth.

"Diego didn't tell me you were coming," Mom muttered, her eyes darting to me.

"I'm afraid that is my fault, Mrs. Herrera. I didn't inform Diego I would be arriving today. I wanted it to be a surprise."

Miguel didn't share Mom's qualms. While Mom and I prepared dinner, the two were arguing in the living room. David had offered to help with something, but Mom waved him away, and Miguel took that as a cue to entertain David in the living room.

"Someone has to take care of the guest," was his excuse.

Dinner wasn't so bad. David made most of the small talk, regaling my Mom and Miguel with stories about our college adventures. Mom grew less flustered about his presence and smiled at his jokes. Halfway through dinner, the subject of Rebecca came up, and I spent the rest of it being teased.

After dinner, David, determined not to be waved off again, pounced before Mom had time. He helped me clear up the plates, waving away Mom's protests. We washed the dishes together, and I showed him where he'd be staying for the night.

Miguel was sleeping in Mom's room, so it was just the two of us in my childhood bedroom. It felt somehow like we were in our dorm room, and in my mind, Leslie or Rebecca would be walking in at any moment.

"That was the best Christmas dinner I've had in a long time," David confessed to me.

I smiled.

I introduced David to Fernando the next day at the park, where he was taking pictures of people and things. They hit it off almost immediately. I was soon relegated to the background as they tried to outweird each other.

David left before New Year's Day. His grandfather was returning from Taipei on December 30, so he left a day before that.

"See you in school, Diego," he saluted me when the Uber came to pick him up outside my house.

I waved as the car drove off.

***

When the first sales proceeds from Margarita's book landed in my account, I immediately transferred the money to Mom. Miguel texted me that she got emotional when she saw it. He told me she had cried when she read Margarita's book, but she was feeling better now. I also sent her the second and third deposits I'd received. When the fourth proceeds came in, I thought

I'd do something different.

"Let's start a foundation," I suggested to Rebecca as we sat before the fire in her uncle's 18th-century-themed living room, roasting chestnuts. "I mean, we can, right?"

"Sure, it isn't exactly something that's impossible to do. What made you suggest that?"

I shrugged. "I'm just thinking. There are so many people out there like me with disabilities who come from my kind of background—from a poor family. The foundation would be to help them."

"It's a great idea, Diego! Really, it is."

"I'm going to ask Leslie and David to join the committee as well," I signed, really looking forward to starting.

Leslie and David were immediately interested when they heard the idea.

"It's cool. I could get my uncles to sponsor. How's your book coming along?"

"What book?" I signed, confused.

"You're always writing something down. It isn't homework, and it also isn't a diary, so I thought you were writing a book. Like a biography or something you want to get out there and publish."

I wanted to tell her it was merely a journal I had no intention of publishing, but then I remembered the publisher was requesting another idea for a book. If it became a hit like Margarita's, I could use the proceeds for the foundation.

"It's coming along," I signed.

"Well, if you're half the writer your sister was, then it will be interesting to read as well," Leslie said. She had read Margarita's book about three times and gave me a commentary I will never forget.

"Your sister is just like you, Diego. She wanted to do something unique in the world. You should be proud of her."

Leslie was right, and I was proud of Margarita. I thought she could have surpassed me in fame if she were still alive. Like me, Margarita had potential and talent. But she was bitter and insecure about herself. At least her voice lived on through her book.

"You could judge for yourself after you read it," I gestured.

"We could also include shelters in the list of people or places we want to help. Homeless shelters, people who have suffered some sort of abuse, and shelters for immigrants, etcetera," David suggested.

"That's a cool idea," Leslie agreed. She drew a book towards her and began writing a list. "We could back the shelter Rebecca wants to open."

That was next on Rebecca's checklist: open one or several shelters before 2020.

"How is Adrian?" Rebecca asked me. "Is he all right?"

I had gone to see Adrian three times since the first time we had met. Rebecca had accompanied me once, and she had tried to teach him the art of macramé, something she had only started learning herself.

"He's fine. He sent me a picture of him and his new friend. Have a look." I showed her the picture.

"Aww, they're so cute," she gushed.

"Mr. Wilkins came to the café about three days ago. He said Adrian is doing much better at school. This morning, Adrian texted me to tell me he wants to be an astronaut. Last night, he told me he wants to be a dentist. I told him he could be whatever he wants to be."

I was glad Adrian was feeling better about himself and making friends regardless of what others might have told him. He told me his dad would be taking him to Poland for the World Cup, and they would be able to see me play. I was on the roster for the squad that would be playing for the United States. Adam was having us practice harder than ever. We had to be the champions this time as well. I had a month before the World Cup started, and I wanted to get the foundation started before then.

I contacted the publisher about the new book, and he was ecstatic.

When will it be ready? he texted.

Sometime in May, I replied. I planned on sending it to him before the tournament started.

What's the title? he asked.

I pondered, watching my friends go about their shenanigans. Leslie was tossing balled up paper at David, while Rebecca held my free hand and smiled at them. I thought about all that I had been through—my experiences and how they had made me better.

Diego's Voice, I signed.

CHAPTER 22

My book was published before I began my second semester in college. I sent it to the publisher before leaving for Poland for the FIFA U-20 World Cup. Adrian was there to watch me play as he said he would. His dad brought him; he was excited about the father and son bonding time. We made it to the finals but lost by one goal to South Korea. I won another Golden Ball. We thankfully missed a session of remonstrations from Adam. Being the runners-up wasn't as good as being the champions, but we made it to the finals, and South Korea had barely won.

My book, *Diego's Voice*, hit the shelves at the beginning of July, right after the July edition of *Soccer America* came out. I graced the cover as Player of the Month. We had a small book launch at Sunshine Café; I had been surprised by the number of people that turned up. Most were either deaf like I was or hard of hearing; some were my classmates, and the rest were reporters and bloggers that had gotten a whiff. Leslie joked that I should make the next book launch strictly by invitation. She wasn't all that comfortable with the media's presence, especially when they started with their questions. They wanted to know whether I'd really started a foundation and if I had recently spoken at Adrian's school, a prestigious special-needs school. I had been happy to speak there.

When I returned to Oregon after the tournament, Adrian's school invited me to speak during a fair they had organized before summer vacation, something I was thrilled to do. It made me feel great, telling my stories to these young minds, hoping my words would be inspirational to them. After the speech, Adrian introduced me to his new friends, classmates, and his buddy.

I also appeared on the cover of *Soccer 360 Magazine*, and afterward, David suggested I open a Twitter account to provide updates to my fans. I wasn't really a fan of social media, but after Rebecca informed me it would help with our cause, we opened an official account for our foundation. David and I had fun scrolling through the tweets left by our followers, and his new favorite pastime became looking for tweets about me online.

He found a few Twitter handles with my name, for example, the_real_diego_herrera, or something like DiegoHerrera. I was shocked to see some people using my identity to further their designs. We even found a fan page that gave updates about my career. There wasn't much news, but I felt good reading it. Later, we went through tweets about me. A dude was asking whether I was really deaf or just pretending; his skepticism offended me. I was tempted to write a scathing response to his message, but I refrained. Some in the comment section echoed his disbelief. One even called it a publicity stunt; according to them, no deaf player could be that good, no offense.

The other commenters were as outraged as I was. One, in particular, surprised me with their vehemence. The person had written, *You should be ashamed of yourself for posting this, as well as for all those who agreed with it. I had no idea players needed their hearing to be able to kick around the ball. As for Diego Herrera, HE REALLY IS DEAF! We attend the same college, and he sits in front of me in my College Composition 101 class. He is such a sweet kid and would be hurt to see content like this about him online.*

David and I went to the commentator's page to see who they were. We were shocked to see it was Brenda.

"Are you going to open a personal account?" David asked me.

"Nope," I signed, shaking my head.

Later, when she strolled into the room, Rebecca told me that she'd found fan fiction about me on Wattpad. Her mischievous grin was on, so I didn't take her seriously even when she kept protesting that she wasn't joking. I refused to look it up. David did, spending thirty minutes reading to me. After I signed that it felt like an idiot had written it, he stopped, allowing us to converse about Arty Blume's upcoming art exhibit. It would take place shortly after the exams and before we went home. The morning on the day of the exhibition, I would be on a show on the local TV channel. It had been exciting when I was invited, and Leslie had spent hours picking out what I would wear in advance.

"Who would want your fussy self as a girlfriend?" David asked out of the blue as we watched her fret over every article of clothing.

"Arthur would." She poked her head out from the closet to retort.

Arthur. I had never heard her mention that name before. Neither had David, as he turned towards me with a puzzled expression on his face. I lifted my shoulders. David spent the rest of the day trying to pry the answer out from her, but with each question, he hit a stone wall. He later dismissed it as Leslie being Leslie, but his uneasiness told me it was gnawing at him. He looked so miserable in his curiosity that I almost offered to help him, but knowing how scary Leslie could be, I stopped myself. It wouldn't do if Leslie chewed me up and spat me out instead of David.

So, Leslie left our room without spilling the identity of Arthur. Desperate, but trying to play it cool, David called Rebecca to ask and was again stonewalled. It was very amusing.

"You don't think Leslie is dating anyone, do you?" he asked me. I had no answer for him, but he was content to stew over it. "She doesn't like labels and feels dating is a burden. She couldn't have changed her mind, could she?"

I left him muttering and went to bed.

The next morning, David woke up with a new strategy of extricating the answer to who Arthur was from Leslie. He tried the indirect approach, moaning that we could use an extra hand with our work and asking if Leslie knew someone else that wanted to join.

"Yes, Miles from Diego and my World Literature class. He's been dying to join."

David sulked for a while before he perked back up and tried annoying her into telling him. It didn't work. She ignored him and asked for my opinion on colors. I saw her smile as David stomped out of the room, evidently frustrated. I wisely didn't comment, although I could see she was itching for me to ask. I didn't want her to tell me what she was cooking up because I was sure I would blab to David when I was tired of seeing him so miserable.

I thought she also realized this, as she didn't offer any explanation. She would have if I asked.

We discovered the identity of the mysterious Arthur a week later. David was already a wreck from not knowing and was stubbornly giving monotonous replies to whatever Leslie was saying. I tried not to laugh or do anything but show sympathy to

David's plight.

Arthur came to the Oregon Bach Festival. He was from Willamette University and had been Leslie's friend since high school. He also had a girlfriend, and she came with him. David was half-relieved and half-angry at Leslie. He was somewhat cold to her for the rest of the meeting, and they got into an argument on our way back from the Beall Concert Hall at the School of Music and Dance.

Rebecca and I wisely separated from them before we were drawn in. I didn't want to be there when they started confessing. I accompanied Rebecca back to her dorm and walked alone to mine. David didn't return that night, and I thought he and Leslie were hammering out the new relationship rules.

I woke to find the two of them on David's side of the room, smiling at each other, and I guessed it was official. Over the next few days, I studied them to see if anything had changed in the way they usually behaved, even if it was a slight change. There was nothing like that. They were the usual Leslie and David.

Leslie still fussed over the way I dressed too formal at semi-formal events, and I shut down her ideas.

I went with Rebecca to a homeless shelter a day before I was to go home for summer vacation. We had made a pet project of making blankets and knitting sweaters, and I could proudly say I was better than she was at making them. Our foundation had already raised quite an amount for the shelter, and Rebecca was an asset to our cause. She acted as the spokesperson. She had been working for a public foundation called Save Everyone before she quit to focus full-time on our foundation.

We switched the causes for which we raised money. Last

month, it had been for children with cancer, and the month before that it had been for spina bifida. Before that, it was for the blind. This month, it was for homeless shelters. So far, we had gone to about four, splitting ourselves into teams of twos: David and Leslie, and Rebecca and me. Once, Miles came along with us and volunteered to help out. His family stayed in Eugene, and as he had nothing planned for his summer, we thought it would be nice to give out a helping hand.

Rebecca and I elected to go to the immigrant shelters because I felt I understood their plight more. Quite a number of them were undocumented immigrants. Some were from Mexico, as my parents were, and others were from other parts of the world. They faced employment issues and a lack of healthcare. Their employers frequently took advantage of them because they knew they were undocumented. Rebecca and I took notes of their needs and committed ourselves to assisting them.

When Rebecca had asked what I wanted the foundation to be called shortly after I had mentioned the whole idea to her, I had recalled Mom's greatest wish was for me to be a healer like her dad. I wasn't the doctor she had in mind, but I thought she would be pleased that I was helping others. I feel if Abuelo Carlos were alive, he would be proud of me. Mom would be happy as well. I wasn't curing any rare diseases or performing miraculous surgeries, but I thought I was bringing hope and happiness into people's hearts. I felt a sense of pride, knowing I was doing something to help make the world a better place. I couldn't wait to tell my family what we had been doing. I signed to Rebecca that I would like the foundation to be called the Bendito Foundation. *Bendito* is Spanish for "blessed," and I certainly felt blessed in my life to have the opportunity to help other people.

Rebecca previously asked if I would come to New Hampton

with her and her uncles. They owned a vacation home there, and that's where she'd probably spend most of her summer. She couldn't bear the thought of us being apart for three months with only texting and Skype as a means of contact.

"We could try writing letters," I signed, joking when she shared her thoughts with me.

"You know what I mean, Diego. It's not about talking to each other. It's just that… well, three months is a long time. I'll miss you."

I was about to ask her to come with me to Sacramento for a few days, but I hesitated. I had grown up in a roughish neighborhood, and my home was quite humble. Rebecca had grown up in a wealthy household like David and Leslie. It had been okay for David to spend the Christmas holiday at home. That was one thing on its own, but it was another for my girlfriend to spend a few nights cramped in the same room with my little brother and me. Mom would probably ask her to sleep in her room instead. I was suddenly ashamed of where I grew up.

Rebecca had been raised with specific standards of how things should be. She might have visited shelters and worked with the homeless, but in the end, that wasn't her world. I was worried she might see me as one of her projects if she came to where I lived. I felt terrible thinking about my girlfriend like that. Rebecca wasn't that kind of person. I decided if she wanted to come to see me where I lived, she was welcome to.

"I could come to see you in Sacramento if you don't want to come to New Hampton."

"Sure," I signed. "And I could reciprocate and come to New Hampton even if I don't really know if your uncle Josh will like me."

Rebecca laughed. "Josh adores you. They're really looking

forward to being hosts. It's always been the three of us in that big house every summer and sometimes my mom. When I told them you might be coming, they were ecstatic. I should have checked with you first before deciding that. Sorry," she apologized.

I thought she was cute with the sheepish look. I assured her I would come to New Hampton. Better yet, when she came to Sacramento, we could leave for New Hampton together.

"When?" she asked.

"Sometime in July," I told her. I wanted to spend some time with my family. I would spend a month catching up with my family and Fernando before I faced Rebecca's.

We had a lot of fun at the shelter. The director was so grateful for the help she was almost crying. We left in the night with high spirits. Knowing it was our last night together for about a month, we decided to delay our return to campus for a while. We went to the park and spent quality time chatting and basking in each other's presence.

"Is it really going to be a month before we get to see each other again?" It wasn't a question but an acceptance. "And with you being Mr. Popular, won't there be like female fans chasing after you? I won't be there to run them off."

"I'll manage without you," I promised.

"Are you sure you'll do a thorough job?" Rebecca asked, skeptical.

"I'll do my best," I assured her.

"Do you have an ex?" she asked, looking surprised that she had asked.

Seema. Our past seemed another life ago. "Yeah, but she cheated on me with someone else. I'm not still into her or anything," I signed.

"I didn't say you were. I was just curious. You're very good looking, Diego. It's only normal you've had a bunch of girls giggling silly over you."

I blushed at the compliment.

I drove us back to school and kissed her goodnight. David was back in our room.

"Where's Leslie?" I asked, signing.

"Asleep, I don't know... we aren't tied at the hips," he retorted.

"Nah, you just text and call each other obsessively," I shot back.

"No different from you and Rebecca. About the texting, I mean. Hey, you want to watch *Child's Play* before we go to sleep?" he asked.

"Sure," I gestured, kicking off my shoes.

One thing I loved about watching streaming services was that I had the option of selecting subtitles in English or Spanish, so I didn't solely have to rely on lipreading to follow what was happening or being said. We watched movies until dawn and fell asleep. I woke up around eleven in the morning, much later than I had planned, and hurriedly got ready for my trip. David wouldn't be traveling back home to New York until tomorrow, and he kept laughing at me as I frantically packed.

He stopped laughing in record time when he saw me stepping out the door.

CHAPTER 23

Dad came to see me the night before my eighteenth birthday. I was sitting alone on the front steps, looking up at the cloudless sky, counting the stars. He slipped out from the shadows like a ghost and sat next to me. I didn't move or say anything when he took a seat. He smelled as he always had—a combination of burnt coffee with a layer of sweat. It was familiar and comforting.

We sat in silence for a while. I didn't think about what he had been doing in the year since he'd disappeared. I was at peace, and his presence did nothing to disturb that.

He was going to say something. I sensed it in the way he drew himself up, and I turned to watch him speak. He had never made an effort to learn sign language.

"It seems like just a few days ago you were five and afraid of the world around you. I remember your face when your mom took you to school. I had never seen a more frightened child in all my life. Now look at you. You're all grown up and no longer frightened of the world. Your mother was always right about you. She fought so hard with me over you. I've read about you in the papers, and I see what you're doing for those people and children. I'm proud of you, my son, but I admit I'm ashamed of myself and my behavior."

He paused to take in a deep breath. I didn't weigh into the conversation. I was content to watch him speak, to let out the words he had kept locked up inside him all these years.

"I know you must think I don't love you the way a father should have loved his son. I was resentful when you were born, wondering what I had done to deserve the burden of having a child who wouldn't be able to hear or speak. We were supposed to lead simple lives in America. Your presence was going to cause complications."

"But your mom never had such thoughts. You were her son, and nothing could change that, not even my resentment. I carried a world of guilt over the way I felt, and I hoped something would be wrong with you so that I could be justified. As you grew up, I came to realize you're a bright boy—so very intelligent! It was obvious there was nothing wrong with your mind, but I still couldn't bring myself to care for you as a son."

Dad paused again, looking to the sky as though he was trying to gather strength to say the rest of his words.

"I suppose I was a bit like Margarita. Bitter, selfish, and spiteful. I won't ask for your forgiveness, Diego. I've done nothing to deserve it. Walking out on your mother was one of the hardest decisions I had to make, but I did it anyway. She doesn't deserve my toxic presence."

"There's nothing to forgive," I signed. There truly wasn't. I didn't feel spiteful or bitter by Dad's actions towards me. I was upset he left Mom and Miguel without saying a thing.

Dad chuckled then shook his head. "She was right when she said you were like her father. Carlos never kept grudges either. I came to tell you I am proud of you, Diego, and to thank you for proving me wrong and making me glad to be wrong."

I went to the cemetery on the morning of my birthday. I

quietly snuck out of the house, long before Mom woke, dressed in my ratty, gray hoodie. I walked there, using the time to run through what Dad had told me the previous night.

When he stopped talking, we sat in companionable silence for a while before he quietly slipped away. I let him go, even though I knew he had questions to answer. He had to atone for his shortcomings, but not to me; rather, he owed it to Mom and Miguel.

When I woke up, I thought the conversation was a dream, but the paper he left behind convinced me it wasn't. It contained his new address and phone number if we would like to contact him. This, I reasoned, was for Miguel.

The cemetery was deserted when I got there, and I passed through rows of headstones before I got to Margarita's. I had awoken this morning and felt the feverish need to talk to her, or needed the physical reminder of her now that she was gone. I knelt before her headstone, feeling foolish for not bringing flowers with me.

The stone was granite and carved into it were the words: *"Margarita Carmen Herrera. Born June 15, 1996, Died July 27, 2018. Our little angel is finally at rest."*

Miguel told me Mom came here every day after her death, even when she was sluggish from her medicine. When she stopped using them, she came every weekend with marigolds to lay on her headstone.

I sat cross-legged and leaned my back against it. It had been a little more than a year since Margarita's death. I thought about my words, hoping she might be listening from the heavens above.

It's my birthday again. I am finally an adult! Sorry I couldn't be there on yours. The World Cup finals took place on your birthday. I wondered if the reason we lost was because you were feeling spiteful. I think I saw you cheering me on, but maybe it was just a figment of my imagination. If you were there, know that I appreciate your support.

Anyway, I just wanted to tell you I finally understand how neglected you must have felt by Mom when we were growing up. It took the talk with Dad for me to realize that. I'm so sorry about that, but we both know it wasn't my fault.

By the way, your book is a bestseller. I hope you're happy with that. People are reading your words. I wrote a book, too, and it's doing well. Not as good as yours, but it's all right. I hope you're happy up there and know we love you. All of us.

I felt peaceful when I left as if a heavy load had lifted from my shoulders. When I got back home, I slept like never before.

Fernando's mom had baked a cake to celebrate my birthday, and Fernando brought it with him as he joined our little party of Mom, Miguel, and me in the living room. Rebecca texted me that she, David, and Leslie were on their way. I smiled at the text.

Rebecca didn't react the way I feared she would when she visited my home and the neighborhood I grew up in. I felt guilty for assuming she would respond differently to being here. To my astonishment, Mom and Rebecca hit it off almost immediately and talked all night in Spanish. Rebecca had been to Mexico. Mom was happy to find someone to talk about her country with.

Mom let us stay in the same room together. I guess she trusted we had a good head on our shoulders. Rebecca spent three days with us before I had to go with her to New Hampton. She had me show her everywhere. The park where I had my first game. The bowling alley Fernando and I frequented. My former high school. Fernando accompanied us on some of the tours and made her laugh by telling her some of our past adventures.

Rebecca later confessed to me on our way to her summer

house in New Hampton that she had been nervous on her way to Sacramento. I didn't tell her I'd been frightened by what she may think. She informed me that her mom was going to be there this summer, and from what I'd heard, she was a ruthless defense attorney. I was surprised when I met a woman as goofy as her brother, Arty. They did have the same piercing eyes. I thought she took a liking to me. She spent time showing me Rebecca's baby pictures, and we gushed over them together.

I spent a week in New Hampton before I returned to Sacramento. Fernando teased me a lot when I got back until I asked how Honolulu had been with his girlfriend. He said nothing after that.

"Blow out the candles, Dieguito," Mom urged.

Even though I thought I was too old for that tradition, I blew them out.

"What are you, five?" David mouthed.

I ignored him.

"What did you wish for?" Miguel asked as Mom served the cake.

I thought about the piece of paper that Dad had left for him. I didn't know what Miguel wanted to be yet, but he was going to be excellent at whatever he chose. I didn't wish for anything because I felt I had everything. I hadn't wished to get accepted onto the U-20 Men's National Team; I worked my way there through my persistence, always remaining steadfast to my goals. Likewise, I hadn't hoped to have everything I had now. However, with hard work, determination and the unwavering support of those who loved me, I had managed to make my fondest dream a reality.

"Nothing," I signed before accepting a slice of cake from Mom.

Rebecca handed me a large box.

"From your admirers," she told me with an enigmatic smile. I unwrapped the box, lifting its lid.

Resting on a velvet pillow was a statuette of me. It was carved from wood, and the U-20 MNT's soccer uniform was painted on it with a large number 10 on the front of the jersey, my squad number. The statuette was resting on a plaque that read: *Diego Herrera, Our Hero!* The card that accompanied it said that the gift was from the students at Adrian's school.

I smiled at the thoughtful gesture, thinking it was the best present I had ever gotten. I carefully picked up the statuette from the box and placed it on the table right next to the cake, feeling happy and at peace. I knew my journey had only just begun. I still had a long way to go to achieve my dreams, and I wasn't going to stop or slack off now. Nothing can stop me on my way to the top, and I am going to get there with the people I love cheering me on.

Author's Note

As humans, we cannot escape our fair share of challenges. However, our spontaneous reactions in the face of any adversity will go a long way in defining our outcomes and how resounding our success may be. When we persevere, bide our time, and apply ourselves to do what is required, we are capable of soaring high and achieving extraordinary things.

Diego's story conveys a struggle that shares similarities with my own. Like him, I faced many medical challenges throughout my childhood. My family received a dire prognosis for me when I was born, which brought about the prospect of an uncertain future and many challenges for me to overcome.

Diego was born with physical disabilities into an immigrant family with scarce resources, but he triumphed in spite of his circumstances. He was aware that education is an important stepping stone to achieving what he aspired to in life. Despite the difficulties that beset me and a somewhat dire outlook for my future, being a child in a single, low-income household and medically challenged, I knew if I believed in myself and gave my all, I would achieve my goals and make my dreams a reality.

I firmly believe education is a fundamental tool for achieving great things. Valuing its importance spurred me to graduate high school early at the age of 16, and I went on to graduate from college with accolades that I earned as a member of various honor societies.

From a young age, I have aspired to use my experiences to help others. I have had the honor and privilege of being a member, volunteer, and sponsor for various disability organizations and non-profit groups. I was also designated as an official disability ambassador for my state of Texas, in which I am passionate and dedicated to raising disability awareness and promoting inclusion for all.

Like Diego, we all have dreams in life, just like becoming an award-winning author was mine since my childhood. We should always be grateful to those who provided their unconditional love and support to us and made a positive difference in our lives. I am eternally thankful to both my mother and grandfather for always encouraging me to believe in myself and my ability to achieve whatever I aspired.

I was inspired to write *Valiance* to share with others the message that anything is possible in this world when we believe in ourselves and realize the power we possess to defy any adversity, regardless of how challenging it may seem. We must always keep in mind that nothing worth having comes easily, and nothing worth reaching for will come without setbacks. We will rise above any challenge and scale any hurdle in our way when we accept life is not always what we expect it to be. Inevitably, there will be bumps along the way, and some roads we embark upon will be bumpier than others.

While life is full of adversities that we must overcome, there is an inherent strength built in those who remain steadfast to their goals and persevere. After all, hardships have a way of preparing ordinary people for an extraordinary destiny. By being tenacious in our fight to achieve our dreams and continuing down the path that we have chosen for ourselves, there is no limit as to what we can achieve.